Julie's Flowers

Julie's Flowers

Streeter and Tang

ISBN 9-781777-366902

Streeter and Tang

streeterandtang@hotmail.ca

www.MorningDevotions.se

Cover design by Megan Elizabeth Saxton

Author photograph by Frank Farkas

Sketches by Evan Mejia

This book is dedicated to Jesus, my Savior, who gave me eternal life and the greatest earthly gift, the 21st century's MVH (Most Valuable Helpmate), my wife Julia Farkas. I look forward to being reunited with Julie to continue serving and worshiping the triune God in the new heaven and new earth.

From the beginning, time has been the instantaneous melding of past, present, and future. We breathe in the future and breathe out the past in the act of breathing we call life. Now we will begin, not at the beginning, but on an early summer's day in 1968.

Pre-Stork Visit

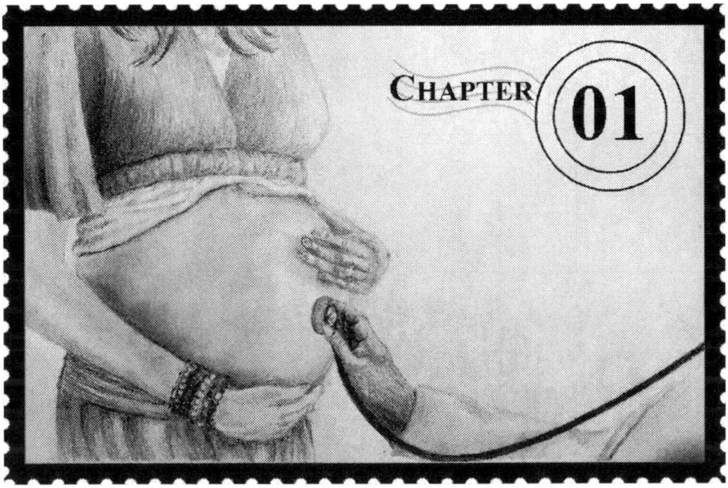

The cluttered walls of the doctor's office seemed to close in on her, and nothing she fixed her eyes on held her attention for long. Noticeably pregnant, Julie Ryan waited for the results of her latest examination. She fumbled with her diamond ring, twisting it nervously around her finger, and tried to readjust herself in the chair as the curved, wooden arm felt uncomfortable to her naked elbow. There was a sense of awkwardness, both in body and in spirit, as she stared at the balding head of Dr. Kelly while he studied the results. Finally, with an air of deliberation, he closed the file and gave her an obligatory smile.

"Mrs. Ryan, there is no need to worry. Keep taking your medication, and above all get plenty of rest."

Then in one quick motion, he rotated his chair, stood, and began walking out. He opened the door and stepped back, giving a sweeping gesture—the customary invitation for a patient to exit his office. Just like every visit before, she wanted to ask questions, but something always stopped her. Did he intimidate her, or was it fear of the answer she might get? Why had he insisted that her husband talk with him, earlier in the pregnancy? When she tried to discuss it with Eric, he dismissed her fears, promptly reassuring her that all would be well. He was also quick to remind her of the importance—for the baby's sake—not to dwell on anxious thoughts. So, like every visit before, she found herself leaving the office still feeling the haunting crush of worry and doubt.

Julie left the building quickly. She rushed to the waiting limousine to avoid the scorching heat. It seemed to emanate more from the sidewalk than from the sun. During this early New York heat wave and at this point in her pregnancy, it felt doubly unbearable.

“Mrs. Ryan, everything go well?”

Julie met the gaze of the chauffeur holding the door open for her, her stomach twisting. “Just fine, Ozzie. Thank you.” But was it really fine?

As she peered out the car window, her tension eased with every mile that took her closer to home and further from the noise-filled city. Eric had been generous with his time and attention regarding the anticipated arrival. He insisted—for peace of mind—that a fully equipped delivery room be built at the mansion and that a full-time nurse be hired. He did not want the birth of their fourth child to be a media circus. All this would protect the intimacy of the moment while providing added precautions for both her and the baby. She smiled and sunk back into her seat, warmed by the thought of Eric's care. After all, what had she to worry about? Eric had thought of everything. It was no wonder everyone said she had a charmed life.

From the time she had met Eric, he had showered her with the best that money could buy. Now life—like the vehicle she rode in—had carried her a million miles away from that young secretary sitting in the smoke-filled boardroom of Ryan Industries. Recording the minutes for the loud and volatile union negotiators was not the most enviable occupation, but she believed in their cause. Mac Wells would pound his fist on the table in a vain attempt to recapture Eric's attention, but no amount of hammering would divert his focus from a much more alluring interest. She had been strikingly beautiful—even then—and despite her lack of make-up and her somewhat questionable fashion sense, there was something captivating about Julie. Eric had an eye for spotting valuable, overlooked property, or so he joked when describing their first meeting. He knew what had to be done, and the first thing was to isolate her from her so-called disgruntled colleagues. He had suggested they meet over dinner to discuss the group's grievances. She had recognized the cliché line but found herself agreeing and wondering if she had been more impressed with his wealth than governed by her principles.

She had been picked up by a chauffeured limo and driven to a waiting private plane where she had found herself thirty minutes later in Martha's Vineyard, sitting in a lavish dining room and being waited on as though she was royalty. Eric had not been there to greet her at the plane, nor in the dining room. During those first lonely minutes she had felt like the object of a Broadway spotlight and that everyone around her knew how ill-prepared she was for this role. At nineteen, it was quite overwhelming sitting in her discount store dress and her slightly scuffed ten-dollar pumps. When she had thought she could hardly breathe from the nervous tension, Eric had swept into the room, calming her with his smile. It felt as though she had been rescued.

"You know, you really shouldn't feel nervous," he had reassured her, without apologies for not greeting her himself, or even being late. "Everyone in this room wishes they were at this table."

Julie was not sure if he had meant it as a compliment or if it was an unattractive air of superiority. Regardless of his intentions, she couldn't help but notice that every eye in the restaurant had been fixed on Eric as he entered. Most would call him a ruggedly handsome man, supremely sure of his ability to take control in any situation. His blue eyes pierced right through you, and with a single glance, it seemed he could calculate the measure of a man. He wore his tailored clothes and gold watch as comfortably as his casual denims. Julie thought he was the most dynamic man she had ever met. With careful precision, Eric had launched a campaign of divide, impress, and conquer. From that first meeting he had established his dominance in the relationship because, after all, that was how he did business.

The wedding had been a quiet ceremony because Eric thought it would be less overwhelming for Julie and her family considering their unfamiliarity with rich, lavish affairs. Her family were simple, working-class folks with far more pride than wealth. In particular, Julie's mother, Winnie, had tried desperately to rise to the occasion, paying far too much for her dress, which did not impress when she discovered that the side seams began to pull apart at the ceremony. As a result, Winnie spent the rest of the day placing her strategically sideways against any number of permanent fixtures. The whole Hamptons affair had left her father, Henry, feeling minimized and uncomfortable, leaving him to fade into the background of the elite well-wishers.

She felt sorry for her parents. She loved them, but more than anything Julie wanted very much to make Eric proud of her. The distance between her and her parents that day seemed to widen as the years progressed. So began her desperate need to impress Eric at every occasion, and with it came a dreaded fear of failure. This fear robbed Julie of confidence in her own ability, and she was destined to doubt her worth in nearly all areas of their relationship. Eric was never unkind to her when she seemed awkward in her role as the wife of one of the wealthiest men in the world. He was never cruel. He simply said nothing at all to her for days, immersed in business until he had time to address the issue. His tone was always diplomatic.

It usually consisted of a phrase such as, “I'm sure you'll do better next time.” For her part, she assured herself that she would—the next time and each time after that all through the years. She wanted so much to show Eric and all his high-society friends that she could be successful, but above all she wanted to please him. There was, however, one area of her married life to which Julie felt most wholly suited—motherhood. She had given Eric three beautiful sons, and now she was preparing for the birth of their fourth child. She had gained a place of recognition of sorts in the Ryan dynasty, and it was through childbirth. The means may have been antiquated, but how she relished their acceptance!

The limousine slowed, signifying the last leg of the journey home. There was always a feeling of relief when the car turned into the long, winding drive that led to the “White House,” as Julie jokingly call it. The prestigious home rose up to intimidate the most scrutinizing of onlookers. It was impossible for Julie to feel at home in the grandeur and opulence of the marble reception hall; instead, she hurried almost desperately up the wide staircase to her retreat. Unlike the rest of the home, the master bedroom and adjoining sitting room were warm and friendly. Light streamed in through the large French doors that opened on to the balcony. It glistened in the crystal chandelier and flowed like a river down her antique walnut dresser. She liked to brush her bare feet across the silk rug under her favorite, well-worn, upholstered chair. Here she could admire the collection of family photos scattered throughout the room. Eric never understood her attachment to old, worn things, but over time this room had become her home. It was a place to play with her children and to feel the part of her which was natural and honest. However, even in her refuge, peace was not always possible. The children's governess, Miss Reed seemed to have a telepathic ability to know just the moment to intrude upon Julie's quiet time. It might have been tolerable if the officious Miss Reed hadn't had such a confrontational disposition. She had the annoying habit of advancing forward when speaking to someone, forcing an inevitable physical retreat on the listener. Julie was always careful to allow distance behind her—clearance from any obstacles that might trap her. Suddenly, there was a strong, deliberate knock on the sitting room door. She knew it all too well.

"Come in Miss Reed." Julie surrendered, ushered in the unwanted intrusion, and prepared for the coming advance.

The governess was more ruffled than usual, closing the door behind her with force. "Mrs. Ryan, Michael has been very disobedient today, not coming when called, and hiding for most of the afternoon."

Julie took a step back. "I'll speak with him, Miss Reed."

"It's long past talking. Sterner measures are necessary." She followed Julie's step back with her own step forward.

“I do believe I know how to address this with my own child. He’s a sensitive soul. Harsh treatment will only result in a broken boy, and I don’t want that for my son.”

The governess shuffled closer. “Mrs. Ryan, I must insist that these issues be finally addressed once and for all. It’s impossible for me to fulfill my responsibilities and maintain authority when I have to deal with these daily interruptions in our schedule. I spent half my day trying to find Michael at the expense of children’s lessons.”

Just as Julie anticipated another step backward from the advancing governess, the sitting room door flew open, and life burst into the room with the energetic arrival of Michael, Mathew, and Bobby, bringing up the rear in his red pedal car. The boys smothered their mother, each of their voices distinct as they talked over one another, filling the room with the sound of pure chaos. Miss Reed’s face reddened as she did her best to continue her conversation with Julie, but it was a futile battle, and she finally left the room, certain in her opinion that nothing would change with Michael.

Once the initial mayhem had died down, Julie sent Mathew and Bobby to play in the hall. When they left, she bent down to Michael’s level. “Why were you hiding from Miss Reed? That made her very upset.”

He shrugged his shoulders, his stare searching the floor. “I just like to be by myself sometimes.”

Julie appreciated that her son was a thinker and a bit of a dreamer. He would often share his little secrets with her, and she knew it was hard for him to have space with his brothers and the formidable Miss Reed always on top of him. But that was no excuse for disrespect.

"Michael, it's important to obey your elders." She took his chin into her hands, lifting his gaze to hers. "If you promise—and follow through with that promise—to obey Miss Reed, I'll talk to her about setting aside more time for you." She smiled, her heart tripping at the vulnerability in his eyes. "Do you understand?"

He hesitated. "Yes, Mom."

Her instinct told her Michael was troubled by something. "What else is bothering you?"

His cheeks puffed out, waiting a few seconds before expelling the air, his voice pitching. "I don't like it when she does that thing."

She sat back on her heels. "What thing?"

"You know, Mom. How she puts her face right in front of you."

It was with considerable effort that she stopped herself from laughing out loud. "I understand that," she grinned. "But you still need to practice patience, consideration, and obedience."

Michael nodded. "Okay."

"Now go and play." She shooed him out the door. As she did, she spotted her new nurse—"watchdog" was a more apt description, Julie thought—passing by. Marilyn Carter was a tall, thin woman with a stern face. Whether her expression came from a lifetime of dedication to her work, or simply a nature that found no reason to smile, she did little to encourage friendly conversation.

"Marilyn, did Mr. Ryan's office call while I was out?"

It somehow felt wrong that in this day and age Julie had to ask the nurse for word about her husband's dinner plans.

Marilyn stopped mid-stride, without changing her body direction or field of vision, and simply replied, "Yes, I believe they called the kitchen." And with that, she continued down the hall with the gait of a drill sergeant.

Eric never discussed the day-to-day running of the house with Julie. All domestic issues were handled through the "appropriate channels," as he liked to call them. Personal assistants and secretaries orchestrated everything, from grand affairs to simple family dinner times, to agree with Eric's schedule. He did, however, always make himself available to speak to her when she called, no matter how trivial the matter, giving her some comfort. If he were going to be home for dinner, his assistant would call the house and see to it that preparations were made. Everything was so orderly and efficient. Even their home was run like a business with certain routines that were not to be altered. Now, her inquiries would have to be directed to other staff, and reluctantly she pressed the intercom. She knew the chef would have been told what time to have dinner ready and what was to be served. He would—if the occasion warranted it—be told if extra guests were expected, especially before her. The dining room felt more like a board room to Julie at times. She was little more than a decorative ornament, not because she didn't have insight into the discussions but because she knew Eric preferred it that way. She hated those business dinners. Her pregnancy gave her a welcome excuse to opt out and have dinner in her sitting room with the boys. But tonight, she was pleased to be informed that Eric would be home for dinner and there would be no guests besides Ron Henry.

"Daddy is home early tonight boys, so maybe after supper he can play some games with us."

There was an avalanche of game requests as she ushered the boys down the hall to Miss Reed for their "spit-spot wash up," as Julie lovingly called it. Leaving the unenviable task to the governess, Julie hurried back to the bedroom and headed for the shower. It felt like she washed away five pounds every time she stepped out of a hot shower. The mirror told her differently, of course, but she chose not to dwell on that and instead relished the temporary irrational feeling of a weight loss. Eric always told her she looked fine, but her pregnant frame left her increasingly uncertain of her attractiveness. She wanted him to say "beautiful" instead of "fine." She knew—if she shared that with him—that he would be careful to change his wording. But he would be doing it just to humor her, so she settled for "fine."

Eric entered the house with his assistant, Ron, scurrying behind him as usual, receiving ongoing instructions in one form or another, while juggling his notepad and briefcase. Julie didn't consider Ron to be a dinner guest. She thought of him as family and enjoyed his company. He was a funny fellow who had the habit of tapping his glasses on the bridge of his nose in a regular rhythm when he was concentrating on a particular task. She had spotted him doing it one day and since then was always amused when she caught him keeping this ocular beat. She couldn't help but wonder if he ever gave himself a headache.

Dinner could be the best of times—or the worst, depending on the children's behavior, or lack of it, and depending on Eric's mood or whether he could leave his work at the office, which tended to mean the same thing. Tonight, it was the best of times. The boys were happy and accommodating. Eric enjoyed their funny stories centered on their antics with poor Miss Reed. All was well in Julie's world. After tucking the children into bed, she headed down to the study where she knew she would find Eric and Ron.

"Do you think you'll be finished soon?" she asked softly, trying not to sound nagging or needy. These were two qualities which Eric found unattractive in other women.

He assured her he wouldn't be long, but she knew the odds. She would likely be fast asleep by the time he came to bed. She never understood what made him so driven—or whether he was running toward or away from something. Whatever it was, it had a much greater hold on him than she could ever have.

Free Falling

It was only 9:30 in the evening when Julie climbed into bed and the nurse came in with the nightly medications that Dr. Kelly had prescribed. Though annoying and overbearing at times, the attention of the nurse calmed her worries somewhat. She had almost lost Bobby because of complications. In the end, she had delivered him through an emergency caesarean birth. Despite Eric's many precautions, she could not escape fear completely.

Tonight, however, Julie felt very relaxed and quite sleepy. Perhaps it was because the evening had been so stress-free, or perhaps it was the trip into the city. Whatever it was, she fell into a deep sleep the moment she closed her eyes.

Three hours later, Julie was awakened by what seemed, at first, like the usual back pain that had caused her so many sleepless nights in her past pregnancies. She tossed and turned, trying different positions to relieve the ache, but after several hours nothing was working. Finally, in frustration, she crawled out of bed and labored to the en suite. Then it hit—a severe contraction. Julie hurried back to the bed. She gasped and swept her right hand across the sheet in search of her husband.

"Eric!" she wheezed.

He wasn't in the bed. He must have gone to sleep in the next room. It was a habit he had taken to of late, not wishing to wake Julie when work forced him to retire after midnight. Now the short journey down the hall was more uncomfortable with every step, and Julie was alarmed at how quickly the pain escalated.

"Eric!" She burst through the door. He awoke, startled and a bit disoriented, but he hurried to her. She leaned into him and threw her arms around his neck as a new wave of pain almost brought her to her knees. She began to cry out in agony—and in fear of losing her baby. Eric called for help. Within seconds, the nurse arrived.

In short order, most of the household was standing in the lower hall. Together, Eric and the nurse led Julie back to her bed while emergency calls were made. Someone brought in a wheelchair. Within minutes, a hyperventilating Julie was rushed to the delivery room in the east wing. The nurse's demeanor never changed. She remained calm as she examined Julie, reported her observations, and asked for directions from Dr. Kelly on the phone. More than ever, Julie wished she had a closer bond with the woman who was now responsible for her life and the life of her unborn child. The nurse told Julie that the doctor had prescribed something to relax her—a semi sleep, she called it—and that it was important that she try to stay calm. The injection took effect almost instantly, but she fought sleep. She wanted to be fully aware of her surroundings; she desperately wanted to know what was happening to her baby. In spite of her efforts, she began to drift in and out of reality like the tide. She saw a blood-stained sheet being discarded on a table in the far corner of the room. She was overwhelmed with emotional pain far greater than anything physical.

When the ambulance finally arrived, Julie and Eric were on their way to the hospital in a matter of minutes. There was a strange reverberating echo in her head—or was it in the ambulance? She couldn't be sure. Her mind was giving her brief fragmented moments of consciousness.

Suddenly, Julie found herself being wheeled into an operating room, but she had no recollection of how she had got there. There was a flurry of activity going on around her. She tried to shake herself free from her disoriented state but to no avail. The last thing she remembered was Dr. Kelly saying that they would have to put her to sleep and something about a rupture. Then, like a dark enveloping curtain, she fell into total unconsciousness.

As Julie awoke from the anesthetic, the first pain she felt was in her throat when she swallowed. As her eyes fluttered open briefly, she realized she wasn't in her own bedroom. For a moment, she wasn't sure if she had dreamed what little she remembered. But the more her mind cleared, the more she knew her worst nightmare had become a reality.

"Eric . . ." She began calling his name, first in childlike whimpers but with increasing urgency.

"You're alright now," a voice was telling her, but it wasn't Eric's. It was the voice of the doctor.

"Where's Eric? Where's my baby?" She began to plead in desperation.

"Now, you must not get yourself upset. Your husband will be here in a few minutes. I've given you something that will help with the pain."

Somehow, she knew deep in her heart that there would be no baby to hold this time. She embraced the numbness that carried her to sleep.

For Julie, the next few days melted into a blur of cruel words that interrupted moments of escape from the unbearable reality. Spontaneous abortion, not viable, hemorrhage, hysterectomy—these words were all so cold and clinical, and none of them described the horror she had experienced. Day by day, she retreated more into herself, and neither the doctors nor Eric were having success in bringing her to terms with her loss.

The past few years had been challenging for Julie. She had lost both her parents and now her baby girl. She had planned to name the baby Winsome, after her beloved mother, Winnie, who had passed away after a lengthy battle with Alzheimer's disease. During Winnie's illness, Julie had looked to Eric for emotional support. It had been agonizing to watch her mother's mental health decline, as Winnie's mind retreated further and further from reality. Eric had done his best to comfort Julie and her mom with kindness, treating and entertaining them regularly at Winnie's favorite fish and chip restaurant. It was one of the last enjoyments that Julie's mom had still appreciated. Eric had savored telling Winnie his favorite joke week after week. He would get the same delightful reaction from Winnie—an amusing laugh—but the joke was quickly forgotten until the following week. His treasured gem was asking Winnie how she was feeling that day.

"Quite well," she would respond.

Then Eric would humorously say, "Great, would you mind washing the car later?"

Winnie would give Eric a friendly slap on the back of his hand and comment, "Silly joker."

It seemed that Winnie's Alzheimer's was brought on by the death of Henry, Julie's dad. He had been diagnosed with lung cancer after years of smoking cigarettes and was gone within weeks of his diagnosis. After forty-two years of marriage, the abrupt separation was too much for Winnie. Her warm, symbiotic relationship with the man of her life had been replaced with an existence of solitude. Loneliness had supplanted Henry as her constant companion.

Before Henry passed away, he had discussed with Julie the void his presence would leave in Winnie's life. He and his wife had had such an intimate relationship that Henry feared Winnie wouldn't be able to cope without him. Julie promised her dad to be Mom's best friend. His discernment was unfortunately prophetic, as Winnie soon spiraled into a deep depression. No amount of tenderness or love from Julie could alter Winnie's thought pattern.

Although Winnie's physical appearance hadn't changed, she had become a different person on the inside—a complete stranger, no longer recognizing that Julie was her daughter. It had been perplexing for Michael. He had always remembered Nanna having a deep love and interest in everything he did. This new person, however, didn't remember his name and had no desire to play with him. Julie had tried to explain to Michael that Nanna had an illness which made her forget things that had happened recently, although she could still remember events from many years ago. This had led to many fun discussions with Michael asking Nanna about his mom as a little girl. Winnie could recall these episodes as though they had happened yesterday.

Michael's favorite story involved Nanna's need for privacy. Winnie had been a very hospitable person, but Mrs. Arbuckle from the house next door would test her limits. She would regularly come to visit and wouldn't want to leave. She would spend the whole afternoon sitting and gossiping about their neighbors, which Nanna didn't like to hear or participate in. Winnie had house cleaning and other duties to complete. So she would give hints to Mrs. Arbuckle that it was time to go home.

"Mary, isn't Fred going to be wondering where you've been all this time?" She would say, or, "I bet he's missing you. Don't you have to make Fred his supper, now?"

No matter how much Winnie stressed the importance of Mary meeting her husband's needs, her efforts were futile. Mrs. Arbuckle continued to have squatter's rights in Winnie's kitchen until the day Granddad lost his patience. He had grabbed Mrs. Arbuckle's hat, from the coat rack, and handed it to her with the words, "Good-bye, Mrs. Arbuckle."

Mrs. Arbuckle later complained to Winnie that it had been very rude of Henry to dismiss her like that, to which Winnie agreed. A better solution was needed. After much thought, she came up with the idea of a secret knock. When Mrs. Arbuckle came knocking, Nanna wouldn't answer the door, pretending that she was out. To distinguish welcome friends or relatives, these were all instructed to use the secret knock, which was to rap three times on the window next to the front door. To stop Mrs. Arbuckle from calling ahead to check if Nanna was home, there was a secret ring. Family would ring once, hang up, then redial immediately.

These fun memories were short-lived by Julie. Her mother's mental state continued to deteriorate, even with Julie lavishing tireless love on her.

After her mother's death, Julie experienced waves of guilt for not being able to love Winnie out of her sorrows and for letting her dad down on his deathbed request. Now to compound this current fragile emotional state which Julie fought to overcome was the third loss, her baby daughter, making it more and more difficult to shed the deep grief that had attached itself to her.

Over weeks that followed, the thought that her sons needed her gave Julie some fighting strength. But it was not enough to pull her out of her depression.

Julie had experienced the battle from both sides. She could fully empathize with her mom's ordeal. Loss could send one down that one-way street called "Destruction," with little opportunity of finding the off-ramp, "Hope." She also recalled the recent newspaper story of the grief-stricken wife who had committed suicide after her husband had left her for another woman. The article focused on the sad state of her young children, who desperately needed their mother after losing their father through the affair. But in the woman's pain, reality could not stop her from taking her life. Her suffering had consumed rational thinking. Death, she believed was the only relief from her anguish.

Julie loved her boys. She would continue to battle this enemy, but she could not prevail without the help of God.

"Mr. Ryan this goes much deeper than an understandable sense of loss," the psychiatrist asserted. "Your wife suffers from the misguided belief that somehow she is responsible for the death of her baby, and she cannot cope with the idea that she will never be able to have another child."

Eric felt that the doctor was exaggerating the depth of Julie's depression. With a dismissive attitude, he asserted that a vacation would sort the situation out.

"Julie has wanted to take a second honeymoon for quite some time, and I know just where she'd love to go," Eric said with an air of confidence.

Within minutes of leaving the psychiatrist's office, Eric was giving instructions to his assistant to get the yacht and villa in Cyprus ready for their visit. A couple of weeks in the Mediterranean and she would be feeling much better. He enjoyed all the surprise-planning, confident that Julie's behavior was perfectly normal and a temporary condition. She would bounce back with a change of environment—especially on the yacht where they had spent their honeymoon. He would try to put business aside for a couple of weeks. Getting Julie back to her old self would be his top priority.

Ground Zero

As they stepped off the plane, Julie's eyes stung from the piercing glare of the sun, even through her dark sunglasses. After weeks in the hospital and secluded in her room, the Cyprus white heat and light overwhelmed her. In that moment, her knees weakened. Eric tightened his grip around her waist sensing her frailty.

"A few days in the sunshine and you'll get some color back—and your appetite. I thought we would go on a small cruise in a few days . . . maybe do a little fishing . . . what do you think?"

Julie nodded and gave a weak smile of affirmation.

The limo picked up Eric and Julie and sped toward the villa.

Eric was right about the sun. It slowly restored Julie's life, and she began to notice the colors of the Mediterranean again. Against the blue sea and sky, the buildings stood like white faces on the hillside, blurring into one another. She even started looking forward to the cruise, telling Eric that it was the best gift he could have given her. When they arrived at the yacht, she remembered how it had felt their first time sailing on the Krystal—the sense of freedom with Eric. Their world had become so much more intimate on the ship.

Then, her warm thoughts were pierced. Loud voices jolted her back to reality. Eric, seeing the shock on her face, hastily explained that some of his business had been interrupted by the ill-timed vacation, and knowing that Ted Harper was visiting the islands, he thought he would invite him and a few of his friends on the cruise. For Eric, this justified the intrusion completely. Though he assured her that it would only be for one or two days, she couldn't hide her disappointment.

"I think I need a little rest before dinner." Begging to be excused, Julie retreated to their cabin.

As she closed the cabin door, Julie sought the courage inside herself to face the next few days. She never liked these overbearing and arrogant people, but on every occasion—for Eric's sake—she played her part. She smiled at their shallow humor and pretended not to notice how openly Ted's girlfriend, Sara, flirted with Eric at every opportunity. Just a couple of days, she told herself over and over.

There were twelve for dinner that night. Between the drinking and the meaningless conversations, Julie found herself a stranger at her own table. Ted Harper was a robust giant of a man who demanded attention, not by authority but by his animated physical displays. His arms and hands moved with every word he spoke. Sara, being quite beautiful and very much younger than Ted, made no secret of her shallow feelings.

"Honey, money is the glue that holds us together," she would declare with a laugh to anyone who was interested.

For his part, Ted would nod and wave in submission. "Well at least I have a gal who is honestly avarice, right darlin'?"

Sometimes, between all the joking, Julie thought she saw sadness in his eyes. Surely he was hurt knowing that Sara felt no genuine affection for him.

When Eric and Ted isolated themselves in the corner of the lounge, Julie took the opportunity to wander up on deck for some fresh air. What she needed most was distance from her so-called guests. There was a tiny alcove near the bow where she liked to stand and feel the mist on her face and the cool of the ship's wall on her back. She heard approaching voices and shrank further back into the shadows, hoping not to be seen. It was Sara and one of her inebriated friends, staggering and laughing at their inability to walk with any degree of intention.

"I heard it was really bad . . . like she was bleeding to death or something," Sara snickered.

"Did they have to take everything out to fix it?" Sara's friend sounded like she was inquiring about some mechanical problem.

Julie was not surprised by their lack of empathy; she knew they thought lowly of her. Even so, she was not prepared for what she heard next.

"Yep, everything had to go . . . No more, little Breeder . . . Who knows, maybe Eric will have to look elsewhere." Sara seemed so pleased with herself that she couldn't refrain from laughing at her cruel remarks.

The two women soon tired of the isolation of the deck and headed back to the rest of the party. For the longest time, Julie just stood there, numb and unable to move. When she finally took a few steps, the urgency of getting to her cabin flooded every part of her being.

Julie stayed in the cabin for the rest of her unwanted guests' visit. Eric's two days of business with Ted turned into four, and he was oblivious to the change in Julie's mood. She said she was feeling a little seasick or that perhaps it was a hormonal side effect from the surgery. Whatever it was, Eric was glad to accept her excuses. It made room for business. It wasn't until they got back to the villa that he noticed how quiet she was. He assumed that it was her way of getting back at him for allowing Ted and the others to interrupt their holiday, and he decided to leave her alone to get over it.

The night before they were to leave for home, Julie couldn't sleep. It was no surprise to her; she hadn't slept well since that night near the ship's bow. She rose quietly from the bed, taking care not to wake Eric, and made her way through the dark house to the moonlight and the waves of the sea. She thought about her life with her husband, working so hard to always do better, fixing her mistakes, and trying in every way to make him proud. Sara's cruel words haunted her day and night. Everyone must have the same opinion of her, and now there was no way to prove them wrong.

As Julie walked on the beach, she watched the waves wash away her footprints, which were pressed like her dark thoughts into the sand. She longed to be free from the pain of them. She stripped off her robe and let it fall at her feet only to see it caught immediately by a surge of water and float away. Without hesitation, she waded in to catch it. She was surprised at how warm the water felt—warm and comforting. She began to swim, with small relaxing strokes at first, but soon she swam more aggressively. The moonlight danced across the water here and there, like hundreds of diamonds, and in that moment, she thought she had never seen anything so beautiful. With each stroke, it felt as though she was swimming away from all the hurt and disappointment in her young life. The farther she swam from shore, the more she wondered if she could make it back, but she was so broken in spirit that she longed for her body to just let go.

The sun rose with golden brilliance as it always did and streamed into the bedroom. It coaxed Eric awake with both its light and heat. He had barely roused himself when the housekeeper knocked on the bedroom door.

“Mr. Ryan sir, please come. Please!” There was urgency in her voice.

Eric answered in his signature measured tone, “I’ll be there in a few minutes, Nina.”

He turned his attention to the empty bed and called to Julie, assuming she must be taking her usual early-morning shower or that perhaps she was sitting outside on the bedroom balcony—but there was no answer. He felt bothered now. He was left to deal with whatever household problem had upset the housekeeper. Julie still wasn’t speaking to him, and now it seemed she was increasing her display of discontent by leaving him to deal with trivial matters. When he finally opened the bedroom door, Nina was standing, head bent and noticeably shaken.

“What’s the problem, Nina?”

“Mr. Ryan, I think something is terribly wrong.” She held out a wet pair of Julie’s slippers.

“Where did you get these?”

Nina began to cry. “The beach.”

“Well, Julie’s just gone for a morning swim.” Eric attempted to reassure Nina.

The housekeeper, anxiously answered, “But Mrs. Ryan is nowhere to be seen.”

Eric pointed in the direction of the town. “Gather together all the workers,” he said, “and begin an immediate search for Julie.” Yet in his mind, he preferred to think she was off brooding about their interrupted holiday.

A few hours later, a local fisherman approached the villa with a plastic bag under his arm. Eric stood transfixed on the package placed before him. The man's weathered hand reached in and pulled the water-soaked robe from its packaging, and Eric shuddered with alarm. It was Julie's. Now he was truly worried. She would never deliberately frighten him like this, no matter how disappointed she was about the holiday. Could he have been so blind—so wrong about her mental state? An avalanche of doubt swept over him. The pillars of certainty that had always supported his decisions now crumbled inside of him.

The search continued for days, but in the end, Julie was never found. Eric boarded his private plane and stared at the empty seat where his wife had been just a few weeks before. His sons were now his main concern. With a somewhat challenged confidence, he questioned his ability to nurture them, but he was determined to embrace the role. He arranged for the memorial to be held at the estate and ordered that the children be protected from the news of their mother's death. He would be the one to tell them, and above all, they were to be kept out of site of the media. Eric knew that Julie's death and the nature of it would cause a media frenzy worldwide, and when he landed at the airport his fears were realized. Some may call it a media circus, but to Eric it was like watching sharks go mad for the kill. He quickly made his way through the obligatory custom approval then escaped to his waiting limo.

It was after 10:00 pm, when Eric arrived at the house, so he let the boys sleep. He would talk to them in the morning. Eric himself had never felt so exhausted. Grateful to have time to rest before telling the boys, he retired to his bedroom. Everywhere he looked, he saw Julie. From her favorite chair to her antique polished furniture, everything reminded him of her. Quickly and quietly, he retreated to the bedroom down the hall. This was where he would sleep from now on.

When the boys entered the study, Eric stood waiting for them. Something important was happening; they could sense it. The curtains being only half drawn, the light was minimal, and there was a definite aura of sadness in the room. Michael shifted uncomfortably.

"Sit down please, boys . . ." he said in an unusual tone. "Daddy needs to talk to you."

Bobby was too young to understand what he was about to say, so he directed his words to Michael and Mathew.

"First of all, boys, I want you to know how much I love you and how much Mommy loves you . . . You know that, don't you?" Michael and Mathew nodded in unison.

"When we were on our vacation," Eric began hesitantly, "Mommy went for a swim, and she swam so far out that she couldn't get back. And now she has gone to heaven."

Mathew looked puzzled, but eight-year-old Michael grasped the meaning of the frightening words. He jumped to his feet and began to cry.

"No Daddy, you don't know . . . Mommy is the best swimmer. She really is!" he gasped. "I know she's back now.

You should go get her . . . Please, Daddy please!" With this last plea, his body crumpled to the floor, sobbing.

Eric picked him up. At the same time, he tried to comfort Mathew and Bobby, who were now crying, distressed by their brother's response. Michael lay limp in his father's arms for hours, and for the first time in his life, Eric felt there was nowhere he wanted to go and nothing he wanted to do more than to be there with his broken-hearted son. In the quietness of the somber room, the two stayed the entire day.

As Eric cradled his sleeping boy, exhausted from grief, he remembered a time in his own childhood when his tears seemed to never end. He had been an energetic and curious nine-year-old, but no more than his older brother, Daniel. They were only sixteen months apart in age and were extremely close in every way. They had seemed to have a sixth sense that clued them in to what the other was thinking—or so the family believed. They didn't always agree, and like most siblings, they argued in certain situations, but everyone knew they were best friends. One of their favorite places to play had been the mammoth treehouse built between three large oaks, especially planted for this purpose many generations before. After years of growth and reconstruction, the structure had changed both in width and distance from the ground. By the time Eric and Daniel entered the scene as children, it had risen twenty feet into the air. It had been July, and the boys were camping in the treehouse when a silly argument began. Try as he might, Eric couldn't remember what had started it, but he could never forget how it ended. At some point, the argument had turned into a pushing match, and without thinking, Eric propelled Daniel in the direction of the ladder. It all happened so fast, and yet he had played the scene repeatedly in his head for years. Daniel fell directly through the entrance, hitting his head on the metal ladder and landing limp on the ground. For days, Eric had felt like he was living in a nightmare and that somehow, he would wake and find everything back to normal. Each morning, before opening his eyes, he would wait for Daniel's voice.

"Come on Icky." It was the name he had called him from the time he was born, since Daniel couldn't pronounce "Eric". But the words never came.

Daniel didn't die the day he fell—nor the weeks and months after that. But as Eric watched him being wheeled home from the hospital and placed in his room fitted with all the life support equipment, he knew that his brother was gone forever. Each evening, his mother would take him in to say goodnight and urge him to tell Daniel about his day. This was the most painful part of all for Eric—watching his brother's once strong, young body slowly contort and deteriorate. The only sound coming from Daniel was the respirator—that repetitive, haunting noise which plagued his dreams.

For two years, Eric diligently accompanied his mother on these visits until Daniel succumbed to pneumonia. The younger brother had been left with more feelings of guilt, because deep inside there was relief that the nightly vigils were finally over. For their part, his parents had assured him that it was just an accident, but he could see the pain in their eyes. For years after, both his mother and father would talk of Daniel's exploits. Perhaps it was an effort to not forget him, but to Eric it was a reminder of what he had taken from them. He became increasingly driven to succeed at all costs, and the distance he kept from others gave him comfort not loneliness.

Guilt could be a torturous thing, and if detachment eased that burden, then Eric would follow that road all his life—with one exception. He glanced down at Michael. He held on to his son so tightly with his now cramped hand, and he knew theirs' was a special bond. It would never be broken.

The next morning, Eric rose early and wandered outside as the sun rose. As painful as yesterday had been, he felt a sense of relief. The moment he had feared the most was over. Now he and the boys could move forward and have a ceremony for Julie. Beyond the formal garden and manicured lawns adjoining the house was a wildflower meadow that she had planned. It had several meandering paths, and in the center, there was a pond with a leaning willow tree and an iron bench.

As Eric stood there at sunrise, watching the light dance along the water and through weeping branches, he thought it was the perfect place to put a statue to remember her by. He had reluctantly let Julie drag him to a gallery once, and he remembered how she loved the sculpture of a mother and child. At the time, Eric hadn't seen it fitting into the house because of both its style and size. Now, however, he knew where it would go.

On a bright, warm, sunny day in early September, family—and a few select friends—gathered in the wildflower meadow next to the statue for Julie's memorial service. The boys stood quietly as the minister spoke, and when he was done, each of them left a gift for their mother. Bobby laid a small blue car at the statue's feet, because that was the one Mommy always chose when they played cars together. Mathew reached into his pocket and pulled out a handful of brightly painted rocks—the last project he had done with Mom. Then Michael, cradling the most precious object he owned, placed a small tin box on the ground next to his bothers' tributes. As they left the service, he looked back at the statue and smiled inwardly. Only he knew what a very special letter was inside his battered box.

Broken Pottery Re-worked

The days that followed the dedication seemed to melt into each other, and Michael felt disconnected from the world around him. The sun rose. His father said goodbye as he left for the office. Bobby rode his pedal car up and down the halls, and the house was filled with all the usual domestic activities. But it didn't seem right to him. For the longest time, Michael couldn't understand how the rest of the world could go on as if nothing had happened. Why wasn't the whole universe feeling the way he felt?

As he walked through the garden and sat on the bench near the statue, even nature lacked empathy for Michael's loss. The flowers were still blooming, and the birds flew back and forth. If he were a bird, he wouldn't be flying—not now with so much sadness inside. He would sometimes have a moment when the loss of his mother would be eclipsed by something briefly interesting, but the reality of her absence would almost instantly rip that away. Sitting in the wildflower garden was the closest he could get to her. Perhaps it was because she loved the garden, or perhaps it was because his father had chosen this place for their last goodbyes. Michael didn't know or care why; he only knew he felt better sitting there.

It was in the garden that Michael first started to talk about his feelings—and with the most unlikely person, George the gardener. George was a quiet, shy fellow. Although he had been with the family for many years, Michael didn't know much about him. He surmised that he must like music since he was always humming some tune while he dug and pruned the garden. He also figured, in later years, that George was a much better gardener than singer. He was always off-key, and what seemed musical to George was plain irritating for everyone else within earshot.

"Your mom loved daisies." A deep bass voice startled Michael, and he spun around to see who was there. For a moment, the sun's glare blinded him, but after shielding his eyes he was surprised to see George standing leaning on his spade. "Yep, she was crazy for crocuses," he mused as he began digging up a patch of ground nearby.

"She liked lilies, too," Michael asserted as if to prove that George could tell him nothing about his mother that he didn't already know.

"And you, Michael, what do you like?" George inquired while he kept digging.

"I don't know." Michael shrugged. "Guess I never thought about it. Anyway, who cares about that stuff?" It seemed so trivial to him now.

"Well you're right about that; it does require some thinking." George nodded as if Michael had made some enlightened comment. "Still, there's no getting away from it—she sure loved her daisies." With the digging done, George walked back to the greenhouse.

Michael was flustered by his exchange with George. The last thing he wanted to think about was flowers.

All that night as he lay in bed, Michael couldn't get the incident out of his mind, and as uncomfortable as it felt, he headed back to the garden first thing the next morning. George was not there. After only a few moments of contemplation, Michael decided to look for him. There was an urgency about it that he didn't understand.

When he found George in the greenhouse, he blurted out, "Tulips; I like tulips!"

"I can understand that," George quipped back, "but what exactly is it that you like about them?"

"I don't know, I just do," Michael was annoyed that his answer had only provoked the gardener to ask another trivial question.

He began walking out, feeling defeated in this verbal joust. Suddenly, he spun around, and with an air of confidence, he announced, “Color, all the bright colors!”

Michael smiled, remembering planting some bulbs with his mother when he was six. In the spring, they had gone around the garden together, looking to see if all the treasure he had planted had bloomed. They reminded him of the colors in his crayon box. When he had told his mother this, it made her laugh. He repeated the story to George, who was sorting through some bulbs on a big workbench.

“I think that’s the best description of the colors of tulips I have ever heard.” He smiled in agreement. “Did your buried treasure look like this?” Grasping a dry, brown bulb, he handed it to Michael for closer inspection. “Not much to look at, is it?”

Michael shrugged.

“With a little love, patience, and a whole lot of faith, she’ll bloom. Yep, she’ll bloom. It’s kind of hard to believe that this little bulb, buried under the dark ground, finds a way to live. But it does.”

George bent closer, as if sharing a special secret. “It gets its strength from somewhere deep inside and keeps pushing through until it sees the sun.” He spoke almost reverently. “Everyone enjoys those crayon box colors. Bit of a miracle. Come spring, this whole place will be covered in them—tulips, that is; not crayons.” George laughed.

“Can we plant them now?” Michael asked with a hint of excitement.

"Nope, not quite yet. We have to wait till it gets a little colder. Something about the dark and cold makes this little fellow fight harder to get to that sunlight."

George sensed the disappointment in Michael and quickly suggested that he help him check the bulbs for signs of any rot before he put them in the greenhouse cooler for a few weeks of "acclimatization," as he called it.

"This way, they get a head start, so to speak," he explained. "We'll be planting these when it gets a little colder but before the first frost." He watched Michael eye a damaged bulb.

"This one is rotten, I think. Guess we chuck it out, right?"

"Hold on there. Just because it has a little bad spot, doesn't mean it can't come back. Here, we'll rub that away and put a little sulfur on it. My guess is this little guy will bloom just fine, maybe even better than all the rest."

It made Michael glad that they could save the damaged bulb, and he said he wanted to plant it himself when the time came. George marked it and put it in a special spot in the cooler, and so began Michael's long friendship with George the gardener. Somehow, all the talk about tulips made him hope that there would be sunshine in his life again.

The sun did shine again for Michael—and all the boys—with the passage of time. It eased their loss, though their mother was never far from Michael's thoughts. This was especially true during those times when family would gather for momentous events.

Michael was particularly happy when Julie's sister, Elizabeth would visit. She was nothing like his mother, neither in temperament nor demeanor, but she was extravagant and full of life both in dress and affection. The first Christmas without Julie was dreaded by the entire household. Rather than merriment, it brought an atmosphere of mourning—that is, until Aunt Elizabeth arrived.

Usually, a mountain of luggage preceded her entrance, and the boys would make a game of guessing how many bags would be coming through the door. Then they listened for the sound of tinkling which also preceded Auntie due to her fondness for noisy jewelry. She was aware of her extravagant nature. In fact, she embraced it wholeheartedly. With all the vigor of a whirlwind, she filled the house with enthusiasm and went about decorating for the holidays the way she believed Julie would have wanted. She engaged the boys in the hunt for holly and evergreen branches, and she insisted that they make a family outing to get the great tree for the hall.

The most memorable parts of that Christmas were Aunt Elizabeth's funny stories of the antics that she and Julie would get into when they were young.

"I was stranded out on the limb of a pine tree, twelve feet up in the air, and your sweet mom, believe it or not, climbed up and—rather than helping me down—she began wiggling the branch."

The boys laughed at the thought of their mom being a mischief-maker.

"Well I just froze with fear, and I couldn't get down no matter how much she coaxed me. In the end, she had to run and tell our dad what she'd done, and it took two neighbors, a pick-up truck, and a very large ladder to rescue me. I got hot chocolate as a consolation, and your mom got a wallop."

"What's a wallop?" asked Bobby.

"Something you never want," she laughed, and the more she laughed, the more she jingled.

Through the years, Aunt Elizabeth became a constant reminder of the joy their mother had brought to the home. Her departure was always bittersweet because the temporary goodbyes reminded them of their permanent loss—of what might have been.

Eric displayed no interest in establishing another female relationship. He had loved Julie; there would never be another to take her place. He missed her companionship, and the more he dwelt on her amazing attributes, the sadder and lonelier he became. By immersing himself in his business ventures most of the day and raising his three sons in the evening, he avoided the dreaded depression state. When it did exert its powerful pull, he would be drawn to the boys and would savor Julie's qualities reflected in them. Eric's goal was to make certain that their family legacy would continue for many generations and that Julie would be acknowledged as the cornerstone of the Ryan ancestry.

Michael was the studious one. He understood the expectations of his father and wanted very much to please him. It was never a burden, but rather a purpose. It grounded Michael to have a purpose in his life after feeling adrift following his mother's death. Some might have thought of him as driven, like his father. But there was something different about Michael. There was a sensitivity in him that was absent in Eric, and he was more empathetic. This made it easier for him to develop close relationships. Like with his mother, everyone would seek his advice, sensing in him a genuine warmness and helpful concern for all.

Mathew grew to have a solitary nature. He preferred to have his hands building gadgets of one kind or another. It was little wonder when he chose mechanical engineering as his field of study. His weakness for being easily frustrated led him to destroy many promising projects, but with encouragement from the family, he finally graduated and took over the largest fabricating plant in Ryan Industries. Having inherited Julie's reflective abilities helped Mathew solve difficult problems that regularly appeared.

Robert or "Bobby," as his mother called him, was the high-spirited, overindulged, and slightly spoiled baby brother. He never quite found his path to recognition in the Ryan clan—other than driving fast cars and quitting one thing after another. Still, Bobby was loveable because his enthusiasm for life was infectious. Even when he disappointed his father, it never lasted long. Eric always gave in to his irrepressible charm.

This was it. The Ryan dynasty at its zenith had Eric at the helm, Michael being groomed for leadership, Mathew as the hands-on creator, and Bobby—or "Robert," as his father called him—making a big splash wherever he went.

Ties That Bind

Michael stood gazing out the window. The early morning sun scattered light across the garden, which flourished in the fresh spring bloom. He could almost see Old George—as the gardener had affectionately come to be called, inspecting the plants for signs of winter damage. Michael had mourned the loss of his good friend, and he had never forgotten the spiritual lessons he had learned in his company. Moreover, George had enlightened Michael regarding the affectionate relationship that he and Michael's mother, Julie, had cultivated during their many encounters in the garden.

One morning, noticeably distressed over an episode with Eric, Julie had poured out her heart to George as he planted flowers. She had confided in him about an incident that had taken place when she was seven. After all these years, this dark, ugly secret had remained buried, hidden from even her deceased parents.

Julie's mom and dad had found it quite challenging, in the early years of their marriage, to make ends meet. Most of Julie's possessions had been from second-hand stores or donated by well-to-do friends. So it had been an extremely pleasant surprise, on Julie's seventh birthday, to receive an all new doll buggy.

Pushing her buggy during walks with her friend, Mildred, became her favorite pastime. However, one day they had decided to take a different route home through the park. The winding path led them behind some overgrown bushes, where they came upon a gang of rowdy boys in sleeveless leather jackets, smoking and drinking. Julie having been taught that drinking alcohol was inappropriate for young people, turned to Mildred and proclaimed, "Drinking beer is bad!"

One of the boys overheard Julie's comment. "Let's get 'em!" he shouted.

Julie and her little friend had run for their lives. Mildred dashed for the open field, where the presence of other people would protect her. Not wanting to abandon her new buggy, Julie had tried as best as she could to outrun the boys while pushing her buggy down the path. She was quickly captured and carried to a secluded area surrounded by tall grass.

One of the older boys, evidently high on drugs, ripped off Julie's panties and attempted to rape her. Being unsuccessful, he pulled out a knife and cut her to pursue his goal. The boys had left her there, crying and confused as she gathered her panties and tried to stop the bleeding.

After stifling the initial wave of tears, Julie commandeered her doll buggy and headed home. On the way, her frightened friend met her. Mildred asked Julie why there was blood on her dress. Too ashamed to tell her young friend the truth, she made up a story. She had climbed the stone fence to better see the horses in the field, and she had slipped and had fallen on the barbed wire on the top of the fence.

Mildred immediately ran to tell Julie's parents what had happened. As Julie had disobeyed her parents, who had told her never to take the shortcut through the park, she believed she was to blame for what had happened. Her mother cleaned her up and dismissed the incident without further inquiry.

Since that trauma, Julie had felt like damaged goods, doubting her value and worth. She had fooled most people, but it was only a superficial, false image. This insecurity had haunted her marriage. Eric could have had any woman he wanted, which had driven Julie to fear the day he would tell her that he didn't love her anymore. As such, Julie had always tried to please Eric and keep him happy. Her only secure love had come from her three children.

"Julie." George had interrupted her heart-wrenching story that one morning with some food for thought. "Every person alive has one purpose, and that is to find happiness. This universal goal unites all of us in our search for bliss, but we employ different means to this end. It is the same desire, but with diverse ways to attain it. Even when someone takes his own life, he is believing that this action will leave him better off than he is now. This drive is extremely intense when we are experiencing sorrow. The good news is that most people in this condition are willing to try novel solutions to overcome their grief. Our Creator has placed this restlessness in our hearts, and it can only be satisfied by Him.

"God's love is not like rape that is forced upon you. It's not domineering; you must freely reach out to Him. It's also unconditional, and He will never impose it on anyone."

George, knowing how much Julie loved flowers, had shared a love story from the Bible. "There was a famous king who was in love with a village maiden—youthful, dark-skinned, and beautiful. The young girl lamented to her lover that she was just a common wildflower, unworthy of the king's love, but he declared that she was a rose among thorns and that his eyes were held captive by her beauty. She'd surpassed all the other damsels and was a rare, prized find.

"The young maiden began to daydream about the possibility of an unbelievable relationship with the king. She became lovesick. Images of her lover were all her mind could hold.

"Then she heard the voice of her lover say, 'Rise up, my fair one, and come with me.'" George impersonated the confident, love-stricken king. "'Your voice is so sweet.'

"Then another sound from behind warned the maiden of little foxes, which had come to destroy the tender grapes, and it urged the maiden and the king to catch the foxes.

"She awoke from her fond thoughts and proclaimed, 'My beloved is mine, and I am his!'"

George then explained to Julie that the king's love represented God's love. He assured Julie that God saw her as an exquisite, stunning flower, just as Julie regarded her delightful daisies. God did not despise her as something to tread upon and cast away. She would always have extraordinary worth in His eyes. Every individual was God's unique creation, placed on earth for a purpose, and His Son was able to shine on every flower in the field all at the same time. What Julie had endured, though cruel and evil, could be used in the future for good, to help others overcome their own harrowing experiences.

God wanted to give Julie a new spring with Jesus as her faithful lover and protector. The little foxes were those character traits that ruin a good relationship between spouses. Jesus would help transform Julie into His likeness, making Eric aware of and grateful for the treasured possession that God had granted him.

George offered one final insight. She hadn't married Eric because of what he had but because of who he was. Riches could be the incentive to give your body to someone but not your heart. This humble peasant girl was not won by Solomon because of his crown but because of his character. Likewise, falling in love with God because of who

He is, and not what He can give, will teach us how to love friends and adversaries with genuine love.

Through many such talks, Julie had been strengthened in God's love. She was able to let go of her bitterness, forgive her attackers, and find peace and comfort in George's uplifting words.

She had also ceased her efforts to change Eric. His inability to love her more than he loved his business would only change if he was reconciled to God and accepted His sovereign decisions. That included his brother Daniel and his fatal accident. Eric was bitter toward God because of the unanswered prayers for his brother's healing. After Daniel's death, Eric couldn't shake his guilt for what he had done, and only his obsession with making money numbed his pain.

Growing in the knowledge of Jesus' unconditional love had freed Julie from the desire to have Eric meet this need in her. The closer she grew to God, the more she loved her husband. She prayed daily for God to mend Eric's broken heart and free him from the guilt caused by his mistake.

The door flung open.

"What do you see out there, Michael?" With his usual abrupt and energetic flare, Bobby burst into the room. He bounded to the most comfortable piece of furniture, threw himself down, and nestled into his familiar horizontal position.

"I'm just looking at the garden. What about you?" Michael couldn't help but smile at Bobby, relaxing on the sofa.

"What do you mean? I don't spend my time looking at the garden. I'm just glad we're through with the gray mini-series you call early spring." Laughing at his own wit, he looked quite pleased with himself.

"I'm not talking about the garden, Lump." Michael used Bobby's brotherly nickname; being the youngest, he had to like it or lump it. "What are you looking at as a career besides travel?"

Michael half expected Bobby to give his usual flippant response. Instead, he was pleasantly surprised.

"Now that is something I do want to talk about—especially before I talk to Dad."

Intrigued, Michael sat down behind the desk and began to arrange some of the files that needed his attention, but he motioned to Bobby to keep talking.

"Well, it's like this. We all know I've had some trouble trying to find my place in this overachieving family of ours, and now I finally understand why. I've been trying all the conventional suggestions, and let's face it, I've sucked at all of them. You think I don't know people see me as the spoiled kid? I've done my best to live down to their expectations. But now I know what I want to do with my life."

"Boy, you're sounding very self-reflective. Can't wait to hear the rest of this." There was more than a hint of sarcasm in Michael's tone, but it didn't seem to register with Bobby, who galloped on with his revelation.

"I want to race cars professionally."

Michael looked up from the papers on his desk to see his brother's smug grin. "Bobby, you don't suddenly start racing professionally; it takes years of training—not to mention talent. Racers have to come up through the ranks to earn that right."

"Look, I'm not stupid. I know I have a lot to learn, but as far as the talent, you and I both know I have that in spades. There isn't anywhere here or in Europe that I haven't raced my cars." He smiled to himself, recalling some of his fondest victories, and leaned back in the sofa, confident in his ability.

"Street racing is a completely different ball game. You're not racing against amateur car enthusiasts."

Bobby was undeterred. His commitment to his cause only seemed to grow as the conversation continued over the next half hour.

"Okay, okay," Michael finally surrendered, promising to sit in on the conversation with Dad and to be an ally—if only a somewhat reluctant one. His brother seemed content with that and headed to his room to iron out the details before the big pitch later.

As Michael welcomed the early-morning solitude once again, it struck him that he had never known Bobby to get up so early of his own volition. Robert had finally found something to be passionate about; that made his quest more attractive. It might be worth giving him the encouragement he was asking for. It would be nice to finally see him working constructively toward some goal.

With that settled in his mind, Michael began going over the day's agenda. Eric would be returning from a West Coast business trip today and would expect a full update on any matters that had come up within the last 24 hours. With a corporation as large as theirs, there were decisions to be made every hour of the day. Michael loved the responsibility, but most of all he loved the confidence his father placed in him. It wasn't mere recognition of his abilities but rather an expression of his father's love.

A Glowgeous Star

The world of form and color had fascinated Angie for as long as she could remember. Hers was a life so dramatically different from Michael Ryan's that—should they be brought together—they would clash.

Her mother often told others that Angelina had started drawing before she could talk—that she was born an artist. Growing up on a farm in the Midwest gave her unlimited scope for her fertile imagination. Sometimes she would be engrossed for hours trying to capture the subtle nuances of an intriguing subject only to find, at the end of day, that she had rendered a fence post. But to Angie, seeing the beauty in everything was just what inspired her.

All through high school and college, her dedication to her art never wavered. Her success seemed certain to everyone around her, although Angie thought little of it. She never painted for money, but money came anyway, and her rise to prominence in the art world took the New York establishment by surprise. It was not long before the elite galleries of the East Coast came knocking. Apprehensively, she made her choice. Once she was represented, she hoped that her life could settle into a more familiar routine in her barn studio. After only a year, however, she was being pressured to make the move to New York. A decision of that magnitude could not be made lightly—not considering all her family dynamics.

Angie's was a close family with a strong work ethic and an even stronger commitment to each other. Her father, Giuseppe Russio, was a quiet man with markedly weathered features, but his eyes always seemed amused. He had a laugh that sounded more like a roar. Sometimes his fun-loving outbursts would startle her young nephews. His Italian heritage brought with it a deep appreciation for family and farmstead; together they were his entire world.

Angie's mother, on the other hand, was Irish Catholic, which meant she was a wonderful storyteller and a born worrier. Margaret Russio seemed to spend most of her life in the kitchen. The other rooms in the house were merely stops on the way to her ultimate destination. It wasn't just a room for preparing food but also the keeper of the family's life history. It was the guardian of long conversations, bygone stories, laughter, tears, and momentous celebrations, all remembered in the worn chairs and dated wallpaper.

Angie's favorite story was the one about how she was introduced to her brother, Francis, when she was brought home from the hospital. Her mother had placed her on the kitchen table and unwrapped her blanket so Francis could examine his new sibling. He paid particular attention to her fingers and toes, counting them with care. Now, upon reflection, it seemed to her that all her life changing decisions had involved discussions around the kitchen table, and today was no exception.

Supper was finished, and Giuseppe settled into a quiet game of solitaire as Angie and her mother cleared the dishes away.

"They want me to move to New York and work there," Angie blurted out then stopped as abruptly as she had started.

Giuseppe put down his cards, placed his elbows on the table and clenched his hands. Margaret, still holding a dishcloth, sat down in the nearest chair and looked across at her husband in expectation.

"That's a long way from home. Do you think this is the right time?"

She wasn't sure how to answer. She wasn't sure of anything when it came to New York. She had made several trips there during the year and found it an extraordinary place to visit. Life at home was like a cool spring, trickling steadily and unhurried, but in New York she felt as though she was on a wild river ride with only momentary glimpses of calm water. It overwhelmed and excited her all at the same time. She couldn't deny that a big part of her missed the excitement and the palpable beat of life that pricked her creative conscience, but moving to New York also frightened this country girl.

"Mom and Dad, you have sacrificed greatly. You've encouraged me endlessly, allowed me to pursue my dream, and financed all my college expenses. It prevented the two of you from slowing down and enjoying a time in life that should have been relaxing and filled with plenty." An emotional lump in Angie's throat caused her to pause. Her tears expressed deep appreciation for her two selfless heroes.

Angie's parents approached her with a family hug, assuring her that no words were necessary. They were very pleased with the young lady she had become.

But Angie wanted her words to be known. Despite the tears that began to trickle down her cheeks, she continued. "Dad and Mom, I want to make you proud. You have always taught me the importance of loving others the way I would want to be loved, and I am hoping that one day I can be the daughter you always believed I would be. New York will allow me to touch many hearts with the gift I've been given and the opportunity to bless others who don't have the unbelievable, caring parents that I do."

That comment jolted Giuseppe's memory, bringing to mind the circumstances that had led him to emigrate from Italy. It had been during the early days of World War II, while His brother, Nico, was the mayor of a little town in central Italy. Nico had feared that the Partisans, the group of armed soldiers fighting against the government, would one day try to remove him from his office of mayor. He hadn't wanted his teenage brother, Giuseppe, to be harmed, and thus he had arranged for him to immigrate to the United States. It had been an expensive undertaking—but well worth it for Nico, who loved his brother. A month after Giuseppe had arrived in Kansas, he received word from family that Nico had been murdered. In the middle of the night, a group of Partisans had stormed their home and dragged Nico outside. They had blindfolded him and then proceeded to execute him.

Giuseppe had mourned for months over the senseless killing of his brother. Nico had been courageous. He had known that his life was in danger, yet he had shown more concern for his little brother. To honor and demonstrate his appreciation for his brother's sacrifice, Giuseppe had vowed, from that moment on, to place others' interests before his own. He now realized that he had imparted this mindset to his little girl.

Giuseppe gently tilted Angie's head downward and kissed her on the top of the head. This was his trademark maneuver—a gesture he used to show his children that he was pleased with them. There was no greater honor in the Russio family than to receive a kiss on the top of the head from their father. It spoke loudly of his affection and approval. Angie burst into tears and hugged her dad.

"Thank you, Dad, for your support. You and Mom are the greatest parents anyone one could have, and I'll always cherish the memories of being raised and taught by you."

There was no good way to say "goodbye." It was such a sad word. Angie thought of one of her favorite songs by an artist called "Tang." She had captured the feeling better than anyone else. That night, Angie sang the lines as she lay in bed,

"There are things that belong together
Like spring rains and flowers that bloom
When children play and the sound of laughter
And their little smiles that light up the room.
There are things that belong together
Like long summer days and walks in the park
When families sing, and the joy it brings
And all the memories you hold dear in your heart.
But there are things that should never go together
No never ever, like good friends and goodbyes."

Yes, the time had come.

Right or not, watching her home disappear as the car wound its way down the long drive filled Angie with a sense of loss. She knew she would see everyone again—and often. But she also knew that from this day on, she would never have quite the same affectionate experiences as in the old farmhouse that had been her lifelong home. The familiar furniture and the people she loved would be there to welcome her back, but she would be different. To think about it filled her with a deep sadness.

As she had always done, Angie began to sketch out her feelings. With that came relief and purpose for her pain. She had known so little disappointment in her life that sometimes she felt her work lacked a depth of emotion, and she hoped that moving to New York would give her new insight into the human experience.

As the plane left the runway and the announcements droned on, Angie took one last look at the farmlands before they vanished below the clouds. She chose to see her life in the same way; this move was taking her to new heights. At the moment, her future seemed uncertain. But just like the plane that broke through the clouds to the blue sky above, she believed that she would find a clear vision for herself and her art when she reached New York.

After several months of working from her lavish Manhattan apartment Angie felt unsatisfied and frustrated. This was not how she had envisioned her new life. At the very least, these months of getting to know the city had made her more confident, and she began to concentrate her efforts on finding the right studio. Just as she had enjoyed her barn studio, she wanted her city studio to give her the same sense of purpose.

The moment Angie walked into the derelict shoe factory, she knew that her vision had taken on new wings. There were so many other artists who needed better places to work, and she had the means to help that come about. Why should she think only of herself?

"Look, Jack. I want to bring this place back to life—to have a working purpose and to be a living and productive entity, not just another batch of industrial lofts. I want it to stay as true to its original self as possible. Artists will live, work, and produce here, and I don't care if it doesn't seem like the most profitable investment."

Jack Larue sighed. He looked resigned but not pleased. He knew, after two years of being her business manager, that once Angie set her mind on something, there was no changing it. In general, being a successful businessman meant he had little patience for those who did not follow his advice, but there was something about her that softened the heart of this strictly-hard-numbers man. In Angie, there was an honesty that he rarely found in others and a genuine concern for those less fortunate than herself.

During the next months of her life, Angie felt more like a construction foreman than an artist. It suited her, though; it was just an extension of her creative nature. Staying true to Angie's idea of not changing the external or much of the internal architecture, the project took almost a year. Finally, the time came to choose the artists who would live and work at "The Sanctuary." It was an appropriate name for the new building. Then, one bright spring morning, the moving trucks began to arrive, and its new existence as a communal artists' space and residence commenced.

A Daughter’s Quest

Mara was mesmerized by the sterile, white sheet. For a moment, she felt far removed from the demons of her past. Rain bucketed down, and the echoing rhythm on the tiled, metal roof drove her back to a childhood memory burned vividly onto her brain—the sound of rain on the tin roof of the garden shed in the back yard where her mother would force her to stay when she was entertaining a male friend.

“I don’t want you to freak anyone out. Can’t have a good time with you around, and don’t come out ‘till I come and get you, or you’ll be sorry you did.”

But Mara never did. Her mother’s cold voice had instilled fear in her—all her life. Sometimes it would be two days before the shed door opened and light stung her eyes. The air that rushed in made it feel like she had been holding her breath the whole time, and she would immediately let out a huge gasp.

"Go wash up and change those clothes. You stink! Just because you're a defect doesn't mean I've got to wait on you." After all these years Mara could still hear her mother's drunken voice.

A defect—she had been called that all her life. She could endure the physical abuse much better than her mother's mental and emotional beatings. In time, a cold, deep-seated hate became her armor of choice. She didn't want love or recognition; the only thought that obsessed Mara was her mother's death. She had lost her hope for a happy ending early in life, and she approached the future as one long battle against the world.

They had moved so often that she had never made any childhood friends, and she had gone for long periods of time without going to school until the Child Welfare authorities stepped in. For Mara, it hadn't been an unpleasant experience to be placed in foster care. Those months had given her a fleeting glimpse into normal family life. It had been bitterly disappointing when it had all come to an end and she had been placed back with her mother.

Ms. Porter had been most convincing to the case officer, who had believed that her pleas to get her little girl back were genuinely repentant. As soon as she was returned to her mother, they would drive out of state the next morning, and the cycle of abuse and neglect would continue. They never stayed in one place long—at least not until she got much older, and by then the beatings had become more verbal.

Mara snapped back to reality as the coroner reverently lifted the evidence sheet to reveal the lifeless body—her mother.

"She appears to have fallen down the stairs. Unfortunately, she must have consumed a great deal of alcohol, and we also found a substantial amount of barbiturates in her system. Her death was instantaneous, if that is any comfort," he said reassuringly. "She didn't suffer."

Mara found no comfort in that at all. She wanted her mother to suffer. Everything inside her urged her to hit her mother just to confirm that she was dead, but this shell lying on the table could feel nothing anymore. If she had suffered, at the least there would have been some sort of justice. Now, even in death, her mother had hurt her with this final blow.

"I assume you have made arrangements. Where is your mother to be sent?"

"Straight to hell, I hope." She spoke with such hate that the coroner was stunned.

Mara ran from the morgue without the sense of peace or jubilation she had imagined she would feel. She had spent so many years consumed with hatred for this woman that now she felt adrift.

"Don't know where your mother kept things," Sid Wolk whined. "She didn't tell me nothing. I looked and couldn't find no money anywhere. Now I gotta go to the stinkin' shelter, I guess."

Sid had been her mother's drinking partner for the last eight years—and the closest thing to a stepfather since Stan had left.

"Gave me the keys to come and go as I liked, and darn lucky thing she did. Maybe we might never have found her. I figure you owe me something for that, eh!" Turning about as if to canvas the room, Sid continued, "I put them down somewhere in here, but no one could find them in this mess."

Mara looked at the filth that used to be her home. She hadn't been here in almost four years, and everything about it—including Sid—repulsed her.

"Then I guess you better get going, because I've got nothing for you." She couldn't wait to see the back of him.

Mara began kicking aside some of the garbage that lay strewn about the floor.

Sid spat a foul name at Mara and slammed the door behind him.

Mara trusted no one. She always expected the worst. Even the occasional act of kindness from a stranger she believed to be insincere. Bitterness haunted her, and even after her mother's death she continued to feel tormented. It seemed ironic that this home, which screamed of painful memories at every turn, could also hold something that might give her hope. Now more than ever, she wanted to find the father she had never known. This had been her only comforting thought throughout her life—that perhaps there was someone who had once loved her and who could love her again.

"That jerk cares nothing for you, you stupid reject." So her mother would rave during her drunken outbursts. "That's all you are to him. A retarded reject."

But Mara had never believed her. How could she believe anything from that vile woman? She was the most hateful, disgusting creature she had ever met. She reasoned, as a child, that her father must therefore be the opposite. Her mother must have kept her hidden and moved around so much so that her father wouldn't know where she was. She had fantasized, in her young mind, that one day he would find and rescue her. It was too late to be rescued, but perhaps it wasn't too late to be reunited.

After days of throwing away the obvious garbage, Mara began the more painstaking search for personal belongings and papers. There was little that explained her life or the monster she had called Mother. For more than a week, she rifled through meaningless correspondence and bills—but still nothing. Finally, in cold resignation, she decided to search no longer.

On the morning of her departure a letter arrived, addressed to Rebecca Brenner from a law firm in Chicago. The letter informed her mother that Mr. John Simons, now deceased, had in his accounts $12,000 held in trust for her.

She was requested to contact the firm about releasing the funds. John Simons—was he her father? Had he been sending money to her mother all these years? Finally, she had something to think about—at least a name. Was her father dead?

In her haste to leave, Mara tripped and almost slipped on the lost keys, which lay half hidden under a pair of slippers by the door. Angry, she picked up the offending keys. She was about to cast them aside and get out of the horrible place when she stopped. She stared, transfixed on the dull, brass objects. It was hard to believe they were really in her possession.

"The keys—one is missing." She heard her own voice of revelation in her head.

How many times had she counted those keys? Her mother would place them between her fingers when she wanted to make Mara's beating particularly painful.

"Four keys. There should be four keys." But she only counted three. Where could the other one be?

"Could she have lost it?" Mara wondered. "No, Rebecca was fanatically possessive about her keys. She never let them out of her sight. Why would she give them to Sid?" After further reflection, Mara convinced herself that Sid must have the missing key. She was determined to get it back or find out why he had kept it.

It took two days to find Sid. After visiting one flophouse after another, Mara found him sleeping on a cot in a dark and rank homeless shelter.

"Sid. Sid, wake up. I have something for you." Mara tried to sound almost caring.

He was obviously unwell; his body shook with withdrawal symptoms. Sid desperately needed a drink, and that was the very thing Mara had counted on.

"Look Sid, I brought you a bottle of your favorite whiskey. Bet you haven't had anything this good in a long time. I wouldn't bring you anything but the best, now would I? Why don't we share a drink for old time's sake before I go?"

Mara thought she would choke on the words, but she had to be convincing. Sid was no dummy. If he suspected she wanted something, he would not give it to her. She was determined to play her part well.

They sat and had their drink. Mara smiled, watching Sid hang onto the bottle miserably and take one swig after another. She pretended to find the stories of their past amusing.

"Remember that time she chased you up the stairs," he chuckled, "and you climbed out on the roof of the porch to get away. You stayed out there all day and night, darn it! Didn't think you'd ever come in. But she knew; she always knew. You'd thought you outsmarted her, but she waited like a fox. She waited, and she waited, and boy did she get you good!"

Mara laughed as if enjoying the walk down memory lane until it was evident that the liquor had done its work.

"Well, got to go now, Sid. It's been good seeing you again." She patted his shoulder, took the half-empty bottle, and began carrying it with her toward the door.

"Oh, what am I doing?" Mara mock-berated herself and held the object of his affection out toward Sid's reaching hand. Then, just as quickly as she had extended it, she drew it back.

"Oh, there was one more thing I wondered about, Sid. You know those keys you left for me at the house? Well there are only three on the ring, and I'm pretty sure Mom always had four. Ah it's not important, I guess." She tried to make it sound like an offhand remark. "Here you go, my friend. Drink it in good health." What she was really thinking was, "Go and drink yourself to death."

Sid grabbed the bottle as if he had been handed a million dollars and confidently announced that he knew where the key was.

"She wore it."

"I don't understand, Sid. What do you mean?"

"Round her darn neck like a necklace. Told me once it was the key to her heart. Don't think the wretch had one. Made me beg for every lousy penny I ever got out of her. Not like you, Mara bringin' me this great bottle of double malt . . ." His words of admiration droned on long after she had left the room.

Mara hurried back to the morgue. If she had been of the praying sort, she would have prayed that her mother's personal effects were still there. But she wasn't that kind of person. All she could do was hope that, this time, fate would deal her a lucky hand.

"I don't know if you remember me. I'm Mara Brenner. My mother, Rebecca Brenner, was here a little more than a week ago."

The attendant knew full well who she was. Her show of cursing her mother and storming out had been the talk of the entire department. He was determined to make her work for whatever she had come for.

"I didn't pick up my mother's personal effects when I was here last, and I also need to find out how I can get a death certificate for legal matters."

"It is our policy, when a body is identified but unclaimed, that the city disposes of it at their cost, along with any belongings on their person, which are usually trashed."

Mara's heart sank. She wished she had watched her mouth and waited for a more private setting to express her spite for her mother.

Seeing the disappointment on her face, the attendant held out a teasing morsel of information.

"Of course, we have been so back logged these last few weeks that there is a chance that her items might still be here."

"I would appreciate it if you could check for me." Mara guarded her tone, sensing that she had to sound humble if anything was to be done for her.

After twenty long minutes, the coroner re-emerged from a back room with a large brown envelope. "If I can just have some identification proving that you are indeed the deceased woman's daughter, we can get the things you need." There was an air of arrogance in his tone, as though he expected that Mara would not have the documents.

But Mara had gathered everything and anything pertaining to her existence, including her birth record. It was a certificate of the live home birth of a baby girl to Rebecca Porter. The father was listed as unknown. Later, after Rebecca's marriage to Stan Brenner, she had been re-registered as Mara Brenner.

The attendant took the birth record together with Mara's other personal identification. He reluctantly handed her the envelope and jotted down the information needed to issue the death certificate.

Sitting on one of the office chairs, Mara unwound the string from around the package and proceeded to empty its contents. There it was, just as Sid had said, hanging from a chain and encrusted with years of dirt. She snapped off the key and threw the rest in the nearest garbage can. In that moment, she was glad that she had no hands. Touching something that had been so close to her mother sickened her.

That evening, Mara stared at the key and tried to imagine what it unlocked. After a sleepless night, she got the idea to go to a locksmith in search of answers. Lock Tight Home and Business Locksmith seemed like a good place to start.

"Why, that is a box key." The old man behind the counter stated the obvious.

"Yes, a box key, but what kind of box? Is it a bank box?" Mara tried to look pitiful, acting the poor, bereaved daughter, desperately needing his help.

"Now you are in luck there, little lady, because I know exactly where this box is. No, it isn't a bank box. They have very different keys."

Mara wanted him to get to the point, but she bit her tongue and pretended to take interest in his detailed explanation.

"You see, we take care of the boxes at the bus and train stations. Now, if you look right here with this magnifying glass," he motioned for her to look with him, "you see a small LTB. That's us. Yep, the LT part is Lock Tight, and B—"

Before he could finish his sentence, Mara chimed in. "Stands for Bus!"

Mara stood in front of box 66. She held her breath for a moment, and then, letting it out, she turned the key. Inside, she found a plain shoebox, and inside that was not at all what she had expected. All she found was a small book that seemed to record dates, amounts of money, and a few old photographs. Did John Simons send Rebecca money? Was it supposed to be for Mara? Or maybe it had nothing to do with her. And who were the people in the photographs?

There was only one person Mara recognized, and that was a very young Rebecca Porter—her nightmare. She had so many questions, and she knew she would never rest until she got answers.

Chicago was hot and—by everything she had read in the newspaper—a violent place. Everyone was talking about the latest murder and the sense of unease for both the police and the general public. Mara didn't plan on staying long—just long enough to get the information she wanted. The room was dark and dingy—not at all what she thought a lawyer's office would look like. She gathered that he was not a successful individual, and the piles of paper filling almost every square inch of space testified to his disorganized affairs.

"Let me see—I know it's here somewhere." Mr. Tinden spoke rapidly as he fumbled through the folders on his desk while trying to keep them from falling. "Yes, yes, yes. Here it is. Rebecca Brenner. Amount held in trust: $12,000. I'm afraid that before I can release the funds, several matters will need to be settled. Since your mother died intestate and we have established that she was divorced, your legitimacy as her child must be validated with documentation. We will also have to place an ad in the newspaper for the appropriate length of time, advising for any other potential beneficiaries to come forward. This is just a routine procedure. You do understand that I don't doubt you are her only child, but due diligence is required."

Mara suspected that it had more to do with tacking on billable hours, but she nodded in agreement. In truth, if her mother had left her money, she would rather live on the street than take it. On the other hand, she took great pleasure at the thought of getting the money that Mother never wanted her to have.

Tilden prattled on and on. As soon as she could get a word in—that is, when the lawyer took a breath—she voiced her concerns.

"The truth is, the money isn't the main reason I'm here. What I really want to know is who John Simons was and how he knew my mother."

"Well, I am not sure I can be of much help to you there. You see, I only met John Simons when he showed up at my office two months before he died. But what I can tell you is that he said he was dying and needed to get things in order. He was a retired accountant, never married, and he appeared to have lived a very solitary and regretful life.

"Why do you say, 'regretful'?"

"He said, he had to make amends before he died, and in that regard, he left his considerable personal wealth to charity. I didn't find this out when he consulted me for his services. Rather, I was only made aware of it like everyone else, when I read of the sizable donation in the newspaper. Mr. Simons retained me for the singular matter, of forwarding $12,000 to your mother, saying that it belonged to her. He did not wish to correspond with her directly, and before I was able to establish communication with her, he died."

Looking about the room again, Mara could believe that the lawyer would take months to get anything done, whether it was by padding the bill or because he was lazy. She was puzzled as to why John Simons, with all his money, would stoop to do business with the likes of Tinden.

"Can you tell me what the money was for? Did he say anything else about it?"

"Unfortunately, Mr. Simons was closed-mouthed about this matter, but I do know that he used a separate bank account for receiving these funds and forwarding them to your mother. Had I been unable to complete the transaction with her, it would have been necessary for me to return the funds to the original sender."

"So, you know who the original sender is?" Mara slid to the front of the chair, in anticipation.

"No, I don't have the name of the sender, but I do know that he—whoever he is—transferred the money to Mr. Simons from a bank account in New York. I'm afraid that's all I can tell you."

Mara was frustrated and disappointed after their meeting came to a close. The most significant thing she had found out about John Simons was that he wasn't the original sender of the money, but rather some sort of a go-between. That put her father one step further from Mara, assuming the sender of the money was her father. She decided to stick around Chicago a little longer and find out whatever else she could about John Simons. He was the potential link to her father.

Mara was shocked to discover that John Simons had lived in a rundown greystone in a questionable part of the city. She told his neighbors that she was his niece and that she was trying to find out more about her lonely uncle's life. No one seemed to know anything about the man. It was as if he was nothing more than a shadow—that is, until she spoke to Mrs. Linsky in 1A.

"Come in, Dear." The woman's voice was old but inviting.

The apartment was dimly lit, and it took Mara a few seconds to see clearly. Dark, walnut furniture with small doilies and heavy, velvet drapery looked like they had been there for a century. Dozens of family pictures hung on every wall, and judging by their discoloration, some went back for generations.

Mrs. Linsky asked if she would like some tea, and Mara graciously accepted. She was hoping for a long, informative conversation. The tea was served in a delicate china cup on a saucer along with some cookies.

"Your poor uncle—now that was a sad story. Lived alone up there with hardly a visitor all those years. Why you can just imagine how shocked I was to learn that he was a wealthy man. He certainly didn't look like it, and him having lived here for over twenty years . . ." She sighed and shook her head.

For the next thirty minutes, Mara listen to mundane stories about how John Simons had always been a gentleman—how he had greeted her with respect whenever their paths crossed in the hall, how in 1961 there had been a small fire and he had roused all the neighbors to safety, how he had helped her plant her front flower boxes, and host of other equally boring stories.

"Did you know anyone who did come to visit him? You see, we couldn't find him for so long, and losing my mother recently, I just want to find out as much as possible about my family. You understand I want to fill in the history. I mean, a family should know about their relatives." Mara's statement was calculated. She expected she would gain approval from Mrs. Linsky judging by her pictures. The woman obviously coveted her family's past.

"I can honestly say that the few who came and went up those stairs didn't leave any impression other than that they were quiet and—" Mrs. Linsky stopped mid-sentence. "Now, there was that one woman." She shuddered as if to shake off an unwanted experience. "Horrible person, you know. Even though it was so long ago, I still remember her. Dressed up like a streetwalker. I think she was drunk—the way she behaved—and besides which, you could smell it on her. I could hear her yelling through the ceiling, and the language—it was dreadful. How a nice man like him would come to know her is beyond me, and I can tell you, I was glad to see the back of her dyed, red hair and that ugly, red lipstick she had smeared around her mouth. But I have no idea who she was. The only thing Mr. Simons said was that he was sorry I was upset by the whole awful event, and he assured me that it would never happen again, and it didn't. That was one woman I certainly didn't want crossing our threshold ever."

Mara wasn't so lucky; she knew the woman was her mother. Between the alcohol, the red hair, and the smeared, red lipstick, Mrs. Linsky had captured the very image that had haunted her childhood dreams. When she was little, she had thought her mother looked like some frightening, painted clown.

Mara found it uncomfortable to pretend any depth of emotional loss when Mrs. Linsky inquired about her mother's passing. Feeling increasingly awkward and sensing that she had heard everything worth hearing, she said her goodbyes. She promised to come again, keeping up with the deception to the end. It seemed to Mara that John Simons was not the only lonely person to have lived in that greystone. Despite all her family pictures, Mrs. Linsky lived in a place that both time and people had forgotten. This did not stir sympathy in Mara; rather, it bolstered her belief that people were never to be trusted.

It took several weeks and countless phone calls, but the cheque from the lawyer finally arrived. Mara now had the funds to move to New York. She had always dreamed of pursuing her passion for sculpting in a large artistic community, and what better place than New York, where she was convinced she would somehow find her father. She believed that with every step she took she was closer to finding him—and a life she had only dreamed about. Some invisible force was pulling her toward her destiny.

Zoning In

Like a paddleboat planted in the middle of the Pacific, Mara began building her life in New York from the ground up. She turned her attention to finding an inexpensive, temporary home. Before long, she spotted an ad in the New York Times.

"Young lady looking for a female roommate to share an apartment in the Eastchester Gardens housing projects, located in the Bronx. Meet at 3033 Middletown Rd, apartment 301, anytime this Friday. Your new friend, Veronica."

Mara pressed the intercom button for apartment 301. A cheerful voice congratulated her for being the first visitor and welcomed her into the building.

The elevator doors opened, inviting Mara to the third floor. “I’m the first door to your left!” called a voice from said direction.

Mara entered the room. A dark-haired woman, sat unceremoniously atop a heap of clothes, pots, pans, and various other kitchenware.

“Oh, blast! What a mess. I thought I had a good grip on it, but it sure doesn’t look like it now. I’m Veronica, and I guess we might become roommates?”

Without rising from her chaotic throne, Veronica held out her hand in an enthusiastic greeting. Mara slipped off her gloves and watched for the typical, uncomfortable swallow. Veronica did not swallow hard. Instead, her eyes flashed with excitement, and she widened her already noticeable smile.

“Wow, I sure could have used those bionic arms moving these lousy boxes!”

“Oh, I wish they were bionic,” Mara confessed. “These prosthetic limbs were the best that I could afford.” She exercised her muscles, tugging the strings connected to her artificial fingers and making the segments curl toward her palm. She shrugged. “No batteries needed.”

Over the next few hours, Mara found herself harnessed into helping Veronica finish moving. Box after box was packed with hastily gathered items, and there was no rhyme or reason.

“I’m a fly-by-the-seat-of-your-pants kind of girl. I try to cram as much of life as I can into every second—as my feeble attempts at packing confirm.”

Veronica was the most candid person Mara had ever encountered. It certainly wasn't typical to learn so much about someone's background in just a few short hours. Of course, her own lack of social skills limited her understanding of normal behavior.

Over time, Mara came to have a measured appreciation for her enthusiastic new acquaintance. She settled into the apartment with Veronica, then she turned her attention to tracking down her father. She had one tangible clue—a print of Rebecca with a man standing next to her in front of a public building. On the back of the photo, scribbled in pencil, were the words, "Mitchell and me."

"Good morning, Mara," Veronica called from the kitchen as Mara opened her bedroom door. "Would you like some Frosted Flakes? They're nice and sugary—my favorite cereal." Veronica added her personal endorsement for her usual breakfast.

"I have a question for you, Veronica," Mara declared as she entered their cluttered kitchen where last night's dishes still floated in the sink. Veronica loved excitement and was always ready to explore uncharted waters or participate in challenges. On the other hand, she had little energy for household chores. Life was too thrilling to waste on superficial things like an orderly home.

Mara quickly got to her point. She produced the snapshot of her mother's picture and asked if Veronica knew what public building was in the background and where it might be located.

Veronica, who was an expert at trivia, replied confidently. “Oh, that one’s easy. It’s the Mount Sinai School of Medicine, and it’s located close to Central Park.

“I love Central Park—so many interesting people and unexpecting sights. Last month, I watched a hilarious street mime. As part of his performance, he stopped a girl riding her bicycle, then hopped on the back, and as she started to ride forward, he placed his hands over her eyes so she couldn’t see where she was going.” Veronica seemed to have transported herself back to the Park and was reliving her experiences. She told at least another two mime stories then talked about the authentic horse-and-carriage ride also available at Central Park.

As Mara poured milk over her cereal, she added her two cents about the horses. “I can do without the smells. I’ve been around drunks much of my life and had to clean up their weak stomachs too often to want to revisit authentic smells!”

After humoring Veronica and listening to her share half a dozen more memories from the Park, Mara finished her breakfast. Pleased with the newly discovered information, she started her ten-mile trek to the school.

At the Mount Sinai School of Medicine, Mara inquired about her photo but without any success in uncovering the identity of Mitchell, the mystery man. She assumed he must have been a doctor. Rebecca was a nurse, and they were standing in front of the School of Medicine. Her working theory was that Mitchell was her father, who'd had a one-nighter with Rebecca then vanished. She made a list of all the hospitals in the area and checked to see if anyone recognized Mitchell or knew anything about him. The nurses and staff were too busy to be of any help.

After exhausting her ideas about locating Mitchell, frustration set in, and Mara wondered if he was even alive. It was time to hire a professional—someone trained to track down people like this.

A few days of researching private investigators uncovered one whose services Mara could afford. Gary Goveno was a wild-looking man who operated a shoe box office in the Bronx. He had electrifying hair resembling that of an elderly Albert Einstein, and going by his appearance, he could have been mistaken for a homeless person. Yet he had been in the business for over thirty-five years, which gave Mara hope that he could discover Mitchell's identity.

"Good afternoon, Mr. Goveno. My name is Mara Brenner, and I'm looking for the man who might be my father, or who might at least be able to help me locate him. My mother passed away this year, and now I want to find my biological father. The only information I can give you is from this picture of my mother—her name was Rebecca Porter, a nurse at the time—and the man standing next to her, who was identified as Mitchell. My roommate recognized the building in the background as the Mount Sinai School of Medicine, but no one there could identify the man in the picture. I visited other hospitals in the vicinity but without any success."

"My heart goes out to you, Mara, not having your father to love you as a child. You've missed one of the best relationships there is—the father-daughter relationship." Goveno seemed to be reminiscing. "I had a wonderful connection with my daughter," he continued. We used to have weekly buddy days, and Rachael was allowed to choose the activity. Nine times out of ten, she wanted to go to the Olive Garden restaurant."

Goveno talked intensely about his daughter, her friends, and her sleepovers with her friends. Mara didn't know what his point was—if he intended to rub in the sorrow of not having grown up with a father or if he was just lonely and wished he could turn back time. Was it possible that he genuinely felt sorry for her?

Somehow, the detective came full swing and related his tales back to Mara's present concern, assuring her that he could track down Mitchell's identity. "You've given me plenty of information to decrypt this puzzle. I've investigated more difficult cases with fewer particulars and have solved them. Having a picture of Mitchell will make my work a walk in the park."

Mara hoped it wasn't Central Park. It took a full two hours to complete the circuit. Nevertheless, she forced a smile as Goveno searched her face to determine if she believed him. Sensing that Mara didn't have much confidence in his ability, he shared one of the cases he was most proud to have solved. It was the story of a wealthy couple, their two housekeepers, and a stolen diamond ring.

Based on his story, it was apparent that Goveno attributed much to the role of morality assessment in solving his cases. "If a housekeeper is unfaithful in the most intimate relationship, marriage, then she will not be faithful to an employer with only economics keeping the bond secure.

"It was one thing to be personally convinced who the culprit was," Goveno continued, "but now my dilemma was how to expose her to my clients." He went on to detail his approach and deliver his conclusion with triumph. He had had his clients stage a formal termination with each housekeeper, firing them but without pressing legal charges. The act had elicited a response and revealed who was guilty. His hunch had proved to be true.

Mara was impressed with Goveno's reasoning, and she marveled at his wisdom. She left his office hopeful that if anyone could unravel her mystery, he was the man. With that, Mara was content to wait for answers and focus on pursuing her sculpting career.

Mercury Rising

It wasn't long before the entire complex was buzzing with the vibrant and avant-garde life that made it The Sanctuary. All the artists, writers, and musicians that lived and visited the studios thrived in the innovative atmosphere. In succession, other derelict buildings in the area were converted into colorful, unconventional living and working spaces. Unlike The Sanctuary, the majority of these weren't up to code or building regulations, but that didn't bother the inhabitants. After only two years, an artist village of sorts had been born, complete with quaint cafés and numerous small businesses. The industrial spaces that had once been abandoned and dreary were now alive with color and activity.

Angie also thrived. She experienced a deep sense of belonging that she had missed so much after leaving home. This community was her family now, and she took great joy in caring for those around her.

Street celebrations were frequent in The Village. Visitors would come for the party and stay for the art. In the summer, customers would flock to its magical sidewalks. At times, it seemed like a giant flea market with treasures stacked from the pavement to the trees, the latter being a great place to hang paintings.

The cafés were the places to listen to the soul of The Village. On any given day, you could hear voices of celebration, deliberation, and political dissension all competing for attention around the tiny tables. The younger artists seemed to have the most to rile about. From government conspiracies to the oppression of the poor, these topics were many people's daily wine. Such gatherings would go on until the late hours of the evening. The more heated the discussion, the more pleasurable it was. When the cafés closed, they would take mental notes of their argument, vowing to resume where they'd reluctantly left off. There was always music playing somewhere, whether from the sidewalk or tumbling down from some window to the street below. It was part of the pulse of The Village, and like everything else about this place, the music made life exciting.

The diversity of characters in a few short blocks was staggering. Eager, immigrating business owners, poor refugees, artists from every rung of society's acclaim, down-and-outs, upper class rebels who had brought their money with them—they all had one thing in common, and that was their love for The Village.

It was decided that they needed to have some kind of counsel to deal with the issues that came up regarding this place—a counsel of fellow artists who would understand the community—and that they would have their own town hall. With so many diverse, opinionated, and passionate individuals, starting the counsel was a momentous task. After days of loud, sometimes physical tantrums, a counsel of six members was elected.

The choice of president was much less controversial. After one vote, Angie was elected with almost unanimous approval. The small, more radical elements thought she wasn't dissident enough to get their vote, but they conceded to the will of the masses. Vigo, a Scandinavian glassblower and the most outspoken in The Village, was particularly disappointed in the people's choice. His congratulatory speech sounded more like a warning.

"Although I appreciate the voting process, I'm my own man, and I will continue to stand for what I believe in, no matter the cost."

His speech came and went, like so many of the heated café discussions before it, with most ignoring his message. As for Angie, she surrounded herself with people who encouraged and supported her, as she had done all her life.

Existing in the same universe but drastically different, the lives of the Ryan family and the lives of those living in

The Village were about to come together with shattering consequences.

The Ryan mansion and Ryan Industries existed as a world unto itself. Like the artist village, there was a hierarchy full of intrigue, politics, and dynamic personalities, and not all of it belonged in the boardrooms. The residence had five live-in staff. These handled the day-to-day running of the home, and were overseen by Mr. Stephens, the estate manager who occupied a small cottage on the grounds. Like the commander of a small army, he conducted his affairs with precision, holding daily staff meetings to discuss events and to address any concerns.

"The next few weeks will be tremendously busy with all the preparations for Mr. Michael's birthday party." Stephens spoke with a slightly anxious tone.

"Busy, now that's an understatement if I ever heard one," complained the chef. "I will have twenty or more strangers tramping through my kitchen." He was referring to the extra catering staff who were to be brought in. He sounded like he was about to continue, but Mr. Stephens cut him off.

"Julius, we are all aware that these types of events wreak havoc on our normal routines, but we are professionals, and I would think that by now you would not need me to point that out."

Stephens was usually a calm man with an air of dignity about him that was reminiscent of a bygone era. His abruptness with the chef was out of character. Although well into his late fifties, he was still a tall, distinguished fellow who gave the impression that he could run a large company just as well as he ran the estate. He concluded the gathering with the usual words of encouragement and proceeded to the study to confer with Eric regarding the upcoming festivities.

"Mr. Stephens is a bit on edge," quipped one of the maids after he had left. "Don't think I've ever seen him that way before. I wonder what's bugging him."

"Never mind about him. I'm sure you have plenty of your own business to occupy your time. "Better get off to your work." Mrs. Ross, the housekeeper, was quick to remind the young girl of where her thoughts needed to be. She was a striking figure of a woman—five feet and eleven inches tall—and although a very capable, efficient housekeeper, there was a gentleness about her that was not typical of most in her profession. Mrs. Ross had genuine concern for the welfare of the young people who worked for her—and indeed for everyone on the Ryan Estate. She had a particular softness for "Young Bobby." Perhaps it was because he did not remember his mother, or perhaps it was his boyish charm. Whichever it was, he could do no wrong in her eyes.

"How is everything coming for Michael's party, Stephens?" Eric anticipated that it was a redundant question. His manager always handled everything superbly. "Any problems that I should be aware of?"

"No problems, Mr. Ryan; I am sure it will be a wonderful night. But I did want to check with your assistant to see if there were any last-minute changes to the guest list."

"Sure thing. I'll have Ron get that information to you today. And Stephens, please check and see if the bakery has the design specs for the cake and if they anticipate any difficulties. I want to make sure all of the details are followed precisely."

"I will oversee that myself, Sir. I realize how important it is."

"Of course you do," Eric continued as he began going over some documents on his desk. "This is a momentous occasion—not just for Michael, but for Ryan Industries—and the cake will be the centerpiece of the evening." Eric raised his head from the papers that were occupying his immediate attention. "Anything else, Stephens?"

"No, Sir. All is in hand."

Eric noted a slight hesitation in his voice, and although Stephens turned and walked out of the office, he could not help but wonder if something was concerning him. Regardless, Eric had full faith in his estate manager. There had never been any occasion to find fault with his performance. He had been with the family for eighteen years and successfully managed not only the estate but also the occasional mishap that would occur raising three boys. For Mathew, in particular, Stephens had always been the voice of ordered logic and encouragement. It may have been the budding engineer in Mathew, or just his general admiration for Stephens' attention to detail, but the two definitely had a mutual respect for one another.

"Mr. Stephens!" Mathew called from the far end of the hall. "May I speak with you for a moment?"

The two met somewhere in the middle, and Mathew leaned in to speak more quietly.

"Before I show Dad the layout for the new foundry floor, I would like your opinion on the two possibilities. I believe you'll notice the subtle nuances between the two, and I would very much like your input from a time management perspective."

"I would be honored to see the plans. When would you like to do this, Mr. Mathew, because I—"

Mathew, anticipating that Stephens was feeling a little rushed, interrupted his explanation. "Oh, I didn't mean right now. I thought perhaps after dinner—say about 7:30 in the study, if that is okay."

"That would be the ideal time, and I look forward to it."

Mathew was pleased as he returned down the hall—and Stephens to his duties. It had always been this way through the years; they had shared many moments where it seemed to Stephens that his views were sincerely appreciated.

"Hey, Matt," called a voice from the morning room. "You're up a little late this morning; too much partying last night." Bobby chuckled, knowing full well that Mathew was one of the dullest people he knew and that partying was not in any way part of his life.

"I've been up for hours putting the finishing touches on the new foundry floor layouts. Would you like to see them?"

"No thanks. I just woke up; no need to put me back to sleep."

Mathew knew his brother's habits, and this early morning salutation was completely out of the norm. "Just what are you doing up so early? And why are you here for that matter? I thought we were rid of you once you got that apartment in town."

"Well, I have to do a little redecorating, so I'm home for a few days." Bobby chuckled as he spoke, and Mathew wondered what was funny. "Seems someone—well I'm almost certain it was Chelsea—didn't like my taste in furniture and decided it needed to be trashed. When I got home from the Raleigh race, the whole place was a mess."

"Bobby, when are you going to realize that life is not one big joke. People, especially your female conquests, don't take your insensitive attitude well."

"Look, life is too short to take everything as seriously as you and Michael do. As for the women in my life—so what if I lose a little bit of furniture? It's worth the good times I'm having. I'm young, and I want to feel it—not like you two, acting like excitement is belonging to a senior's coffee club."

"Who's a senior citizen?" Michael asked, as he entered the room, and the three settled into their usual bickering over breakfast.

Through the laughter, however, there was genuine concern that their little brother was living a little too close to the edge. Perhaps he should be more concerned about the consequences of his actions. This was particularly true when it came to racing. He was increasingly disliked by the other competitors, who believed his careless and sometimes dangerous maneuvers were directly related to his family's money. All this worried Michael, but whenever he tried to talk to Bobby—or his father—they both had an indifferent attitude, chalking it up to youth. Sometimes Michael wondered if perhaps he worried too much and that it might have something to do with his mother's accident. Whatever the reason, he felt the weight of worry, and sometimes he wished he could be as dismissive as others in the family.

That evening, Mathew presented the layout for the new foundry floor to Stephens, but he sensed something deeper was on the man's mind.

"I've known you too long, Mr. Stephens, not to know that something is bothering you. You're having difficulty really concentrating on my plans. Can you tell me what your concern is?" Mathew inquired.

"I'm sorry for not giving you my undivided attention, Mr. Mathew, and you are right; something is upsetting me. But it's not my place to share my personal feelings on this matter."

“What matter?” Mathew asked, wondering what had caused Stephens so much turmoil. “I give you permission to speak from your heart, and of course, this will be off the record. Don’t feel you’ll be reprimanded for any critical expressed feelings.” Mathew assured Stephens that he wanted to know what was troubling him.

Stephens commenced his speech. “Mr. Ryan is ecstatic about the announcement of the new foundry at Michael’s birthday party, with the foundry-shaped cake representing the beginning of moving forward with the project. But I’ve heard rumors that the radical wing of artists is at the point of considering mob tactics to prevent Ryan Industries from taking possession of their ‘Village.’ I fear for your lives, and I know if I told Mr. Ryan this, it would only embolden him to meet the challenge head-on, fighting fire with fire. I believe it would be much better for the whole community if some compromise could be made. It would earn us some good will over this intense controversy.” Stephens sat down, placing his hands on his forehead.

“I agree with you, Mr. Stephens, and not only me, but Michael too. He has already talked to Dad about our image being tarnished by our so-called bully tactics over these struggling artists. But you know as well as I do that Dad has never backed down from any controversy. He always plays to win, and the word ‘compromise’ isn’t in his vocabulary. The best we can do is hope that some circumstance could do the impossible and change his heart.”

Stephens was comforted to know that he had allies, even though he knew the inevitable would happen. He snapped out of his depression and addressed Mathew. "You are correct, Mr. Mathew, so let's move on. Show me those plans again, and I'll give my thoughts on what changes you should make in your presentation to Mr. Ryan."

Opposites Attract

Veronica, knowing that Mara was searching for work in the sculpting field, researched a group of artists that had been rejuvenating the city in an area called The Village. She explained to Mara that the artists both lived and worked right in the area. Angie Russio was the driving force behind the group, and she was open to helping young artists become established.

"I would hate to see you leave me, Mara, but I know it would be a great place to begin your career as a sculptor. All you need to do is contact The Sanctuary and ask for an interview to become a member.

Mara was thrilled with Veronica's suggestion and immediately looked into it. After a few inquiries, she was able to set up an appointment with Angie Russio to apply for residency at The Sanctuary as a metal sculptress.

Mara arrived at The Sanctuary, sat in the corner of the reception area, and waited for her interview. She rocked her knees nervously and twiddled her artificial fingers beneath her gloves. She had little confidence that she would receive positive feedback from the other artists. Her work was so untraditional. She had never attended a prestigious art school or received professional training. She had simply been taught welding by her stepdad, Stan Brenner, and had gravitated to metal sculpting as an outlet for her pain and loneliness. Shaping iron and steel into her creations gave Mara a sense of strength and the feeling of being in control. Yet there had never been any hope of nurturing these qualities in Rebecca's presence. She had always criticized Mara forcefully.

One particularly vivid memory came to mind. It was the Mother's Day shortly after Rebecca's divorce to Stan Brenner, and Mara had decided to make her mother a metal flower. Instead of receiving a "thank you," Mara was humiliated when a drunken Rebecca tossed the gift out the window, cursing her ex-husband and swearing that she never wanted to be reminded of him again.

"If you have time to do this kind of garbage, then you have time to get a job and start paying for your keep," Rebecca had warned Mara.

From that time on, Mara had cautiously pursued her passion in isolation at secondary school, being careful not to rouse Rebecca's suspicions.

Angie's voice cut into Mara's flashbacks. "Welcome to The Sanctuary! You must be Mara Brenner. Come on back here to my office, and we'll get started."

Though fearful of the meeting's outcome, Mara wanted to give it her best. After a few minutes of small talk, Angie asked to see Mara's portfolio. Not realizing that she needed one, Mara saw that she was in over her head and wouldn't be able to convince a professional artist of her talent.

"I'm sorry, Miss Russio. I don't have a portfolio, and I apologize for wasting your time."

As Mara slowly turned to the door, Angie grabbed her by the forearms. She was now aware of Mara's prosthetic limbs, and yet she continued to hold on. Gently, she convinced Mara to stay and chat over some tea. Mara was captivated by Angie's compassion. In her experience, when people discovered her disability, they would quickly withdraw, feeling awkward and not knowing how to respond.

"How did you come to work in metal? I would have thought that another medium might have been easier. Oh, I hope you don't mind me asking?" Angie stammered. "I'm sorry—it is the country in me, I guess. I just say what I'm thinking, and sometimes it gets me in trouble."

Mara smiled, amused by her honesty. "No, I like it. People always tiptoe around me, pretending they don't see anything wrong. I never felt like I fit in anywhere—until I started to do this—and I started quite unintentionally.

"You see," Mara went on, "my stepfather was a welder, and one day, when he'd had a couple of beers too many, he thought it would be a great idea to teach me to weld. He thought I'd better learn to look after myself, seeing as my chances of finding a man were slim. Funny thing was, I took to it right away, and before long there was nothing left he could teach me.

"I wanted to do more than just straight welding; I wanted to create something. Pieces that said, 'hey, this is me. Maybe I don't look like everyone else, but I've got something to say, and I want you to listen.' I know that to some people my work may be ugly, and it may make them uncomfortable, but as long as they take a look—a long, hard look—then I feel that my pieces have served their purpose. Sometimes we need to make people acknowledge the truth."

After Mara had opened up, she explained that all her work was in a large, rented garage back in Bloomfield, Connecticut. She had only brought this small, iron rod flower to show Angie.

Angie's eyes widened. "That is so original and eye catching. It's marvelous! I've got to see your whole collection." Angie's next words astounded Mara. "You haven't wasted my time, Mara, you have intrigued me. Tomorrow we're going on a road trip, so get packed. We're heading to Bloomfield to see the rest of your work.

Emotionally gripped by the warmth Angie showed her, Mara took a little time to compose herself. Then she forced out the words, "Thank you so much, Miss Russio."

"Call me Angie. We're not strangers; we're friends."

The next morning, Angie pulled up to Mara's apartment in a Ford pick-up truck. The two-toned blue finish was scratched in multiple places, and the frame sported some serious dents. Leaning over, Angie shoved the passenger door open, greeting Mara with a friendly smile. "I hope you like coffee and donuts?"

Mara awkwardly struggled up onto the seat, covered with a vintage, black-and-gray blanket. After taking hold of the coffee, she saw her reflection in Angie's aviator sunglasses and noticed a small smile on her face. It was then that she realized that some of her nerves were slowly turning into excitement.

"I'm confident that your sculptures will impress me, Mara, so I wanted to help transport your work back to The Sanctuary."

"But you've only seen a tiny piece of it. I'm afraid it might let you down and you won't find the value you're expecting." Mara sought to lower Angie's expectations.

"If that's the case, you've got a free trip and gained a new friend. It's a win-win situation, so let's enjoy our time together."

Mara had never met anyone like Angie in her life. It was difficult for her to believe that there were people without hidden agendas.

During the drive, Angie shared more about her life, the acquisition of the old shoe factory, the growth of the artist colony, and the present danger of Ryan Industries' new foundry replacing The Village. Mara asked about the negotiations with the corporate giant. Angie revealed all the details, including her discussions with Michael, the son of Eric Ryan.

"Are you attracted to Michael, Angie?" Mara inquired curiously.

"Yes, he is very good looking," Angie confessed. "But I could never date someone who can't see the value in art. Besides, the colony is my life, and who has time to date, anyway? I left a small town and a loving family to pursue success in something I'm passionate about, and I don't want to let my parents down. They've sacrificed to allow me my dream."

"We're here!" Mara declared. "Just around that bend at the end of the street you'll see the large garage. It's actually a barn."

Angie was awestruck as she observed the sight. The neighborhood consisted mostly of apartment buildings, but where the street came to a dead end, there was a large piece of property that looked like it belonged to some disordered clan in the Ozark Mountains! A high fence surrounded the compound with a sign that read, "Keep out, if you value your life." The huge acreage was a junkyard full of old car parts and household appliances, overgrown grass, and a monstrous, eclectic barn with multicolored shingles. It looked like the building had been thrown together from junk found on the premises.

"We lived down the street, and my stepdad, Stan, used to rent this garage to do his welding in. It's owned by a couple of eccentric brothers, Larry and Gary, who are extremely anti-government, which explains the threatening signs. I started renting the garage a couple of years ago, as the rent was cheap and no one bothers you out here."

From the corner of her eye, Angie spotted an old man with a clubfoot and a patch over his right eye watching them.

"Don't worry," Mara assured her. "As long as you don't look like a governmental agent, you're fine. Follow me." Mara ushered Angie on, and they worked their way through the junkyard toward the barn, passing a labyrinth of scrap metal car parts piled on top of each other.

Having entered the dim, gloomy barn, Mara slipped away from Angie and flipped the power switch, which resonated in the dark. Fluorescent lights popped and hummed, flickering on to reveal a sea of sculptures.

Mara stood on a grated stairwell and watched as Angie walked up to each piece, circling her way around the welding floor. When she reached her original position, she stood there, motionless, staring at the sculptures with her back to Mara.

Mara's fear of rejection morphed into reality before her very eyes. Angie remained silent. She didn't like Mara's work, and she was formulating a polite way to turn her down. Mara braced herself as Angie slowly turned to face her.

"Mara, what can I say to do your art justice?" Tears were streaming down Angie's face. No critic, collector, or art lover could come close to describing the honesty, the rawness, the pain, the fragility, the vulnerability your pieces show, one after another. It is outrageous to hide these away in a barn. Who could imagine that such talent lay hidden here? Mara, we have to share this with the art world. We have to share you . . . You are a hidden gem!"

Mara bounced down the stairwell. She had tears in her eyes as she embraced Angie. "No one has ever given me such wonderful encouragement. Thank you, Angie!"

Mara's collection was too large for Angie's pick-up.

"I notice that Larry and Gary have a crane out back," Angie mused. "Do you think we could hire them to transport your whole collection to The Sanctuary?"

"Well, let's go and ask them. I'm sure they never turn down opportunities to make money," Mara confidently replied.

Larry and Gary gladly accepted. Much labor would be required to clear a path from the barn to the moving van. So Angie and Mara gave themselves a three-month timeline to prepare for Mara's coming-out event. It would be the big debut to her career—her private showing of her works. In the meantime, the brothers had plenty of time to deliver the collection.

Angie was ecstatic over Mara's potential as a sculpture artist. More thrilling still was her plan to promote Mara as the face of Sanctuary—their poster artist, especially now, while entrenched in their battle with Ryan Industries. Her work was brilliant, and all of it had been crafted in solitude. Mara could rise from obscurity to be the inspiration for all disabled individuals, many of whom believed that their talent would be undervalued because of their impairment. The message of her national art campaign could motivate others to dream their future into reality, "If you can dream it, you can do it."

Angie's concern was that Ryan Industries, who had the New York bankers in their back pocket, would eventually get them to call in the artists' loans on all their building mortgages. Although the colony was successful, they were still in the fledgling stage of their development, and they weren't in a position to repay entire debts. However, if the public became enthralled with Mara and her rise to success despite the odds she had battled, they could not and would not allow Ryan Industries to replace The Village with a foundry. Wealthy art lovers would come to the defense of this underdog—the insignificant over the mammoth bully—and these activists would be difficult to defeat, even for Eric Ryan.

Angie's idea was to host a gala to raise money for the artist colony and to auction off a piece of Mara's work. She hoped that all the heads of industries would attend and compete to purchase Mara's donated sculpture and that it would be displayed as public art at one of their headquarters. If these affluent art lovers were swayed onto the Mara bandwagon, they would certainly counterbalance the New York bankers and Ryan Industries regarding the bank loans.

On the ride back to New York, Angie shared with Mara her ideas to make her a superstar in the art world. Mara was conflicted. She appreciated Angie's kindness and faith in her talent, but being up front in the public eye would be frightening. She didn't know how to handle the limelight like a professional. And yet she didn't want to let Angie down.

Big Game Hunting

As the Ryan-Sanctuary war continued to heat up, rumors reached Ryan Industries that the artists were through with negotiating and that if Goliath didn't back down, casualties would come shortly. The threats became reality much sooner than expected, and the youngest Ryan was the first victim.

During Bobby's morning practice run, when he was on his third lap, his brakes failed, and his vehicle careened into the wall. Bobby was rushed to Bellevue Hospital Center, and Eric was notified. When Eric arrived, he was told that Bobby had several injuries, including a concussion, broken ribs, and a ruptured spleen. He needed immediate surgery.

As the family waited for Bobby to come out of surgery, Eric spewed out his frustration to his sons.

"It's those unhinged artists who did this, and I'm going to make sure they get what they deserve."

"Wait, Dad," said Michael. "Don't jump to conclusions. We don't know who's responsible. Let's just hope Bobby is going to be alright." He tried to steer Eric's concerns toward Bobby and away from avenging his violators.

"Dad," Mathew added, "we can't be sure who did this until the accident is investigated."

"I'm going to hire my own investigators. I don't have the time to wait for the police's lethargic attempt to round up these criminals."

The boys realized that their efforts to calm their dad were futile, so they remained silent and let him rant.

It's all because those artists can't accept our new foundry taking up their space. Especially, they can't accept progress. They're lazy, stubborn, childish individuals who are going to lose in the end—especially those responsible for attempting to kill Robert."

The surgeon entered the room, bringing Eric's tirade to a standstill. He and his two eldest sons leaned in, waiting with bated breath to hear the outcome of the operation.

"Mr. Ryan, the surgery was successful. We did a partial splenectomy, which will allow the spleen to continue to function and reduce the risk of infection. Robert is in recovery now, although we are going to monitor his concussion, and he will be quite uncomfortable while his broken ribs begin to heal. He also has a herniated disc that may need surgery if it does not respond to treatment."

Eric was encouraged by the surgeon's report. "Thank you, Dr. Gold. Our family is grateful to you for coming and operating on Robert immediately. We have heard that you are the best in your field, but your services are very difficult to procure since you are in such demand."

Dr. Gold bent his head downward. "Saving lives is what I live to do."

"About how long do you think Robert will be in the hospital?" Eric inquired.

Dr. Gold looked at his chart. "We may keep him a little longer than usual, just to make certain there are no side effects. The force of the crash was strong, and our bodies are not made for the type of impact that Robert experienced. We need to take precautions and make sure that he does not have any other injuries that we have not yet detected. Many people believe that a head-on collision at the same speed would be twice as bad as running into a solid wall, but that is a myth. They would both produce the same amount of force. In fact, the wall may generate slightly more force because of its consistency in comparison to a vehicle's composition. Let's take it one day at a time, and hopefully Robert will respond. He is a healthy, young man; he has that going for him."

Eric concluded his conversation with Dr. Gold then assured his sons that he would find the artists who'd attempted to take Robert's life.

Mathew put a hand on his father's shoulder. "Dad, you've been living in the tension of the Sanctuary war. You have an ever-present expectation that something is about to happen. Your stress has made you quick to conclude that the accident was a conspiracy."

Michael agreed with Mathew's assessment. Bobby was an easy target. He was already destroying himself with his daring and reckless lifestyle. Loving fast cars and womanizing would make it difficult for the authorities to track down his perpetrator. Many jilted women and disgruntled race car drivers had legitimate motives to lash out at Bobby. It wasn't certain that any Village artist was behind this crime.

A thorough inspection was conducted on Bobby's vehicle. The cause of the accident was confirmed to be brake failure. A foreign substance had been added to the brake fluid to lower its boiling point. As Bobby had reached high speeds, his brakes required maximum pressure, causing them to heat up. Since the boiling point of the fluid had been lowered, the mixture had boiled, which had caused gas pockets. And with gas pockets, the brakes didn't function.

This type of tampering was challenging to identify; brake fluid cooled quickly, making everything look normal. The person responsible for the crime would have had no trouble implementing the plan and little worry about being caught. If it weren't for Bobby having so many enemies, this incident could have easily been written off as a mechanical failure.

Although Eric worried that fighting back could place his other children in danger, it was not in his character to back down from a challenge. It was time to take action in the offensive. He hired a team of private investigators to hunt down the culprits and have them put away for life.

The East Coast Intelligence Agency was recognized as the best investigating team in the country. Eric hired two of their employees to pose as artists to work within The Village and gain intelligence on Bobby's accident and any future moves planned against the Ryan family. There existed a small clique of far-left artists that were verbally abusive toward Ryan Industries, but most felt this group would never promote the physical harming of the members of the Ryan family.

Generally, the Village inhabitants were peaceful, non-aggressive, and opposed to violence. The consensus amongst the residents was that only one artist was capable of such retaliation: Vigo, the glassblower. Although there was no first-hand proof of his guilt, many agreed that he had the courage and temperament to defend his livelihood. Most of the conservative artists, including Angie Russio, believed that negotiations were the best way to proceed and that violence was not an option. However, this frustrated the liberal artists, who saw that these meetings were going nowhere and that in time they would lose their community.

A month later, Mathew became the next victim. A phony memo was sent to him about meeting Jack LaRue, Angie's business manager, to discuss his engineering plans for the new foundry. Mathew was to meet Jack at 7:00 pm at The

Sanctuary. Prior to the meeting, someone chipped off a large piece of the upper floor architectural design from the outside of the building near a window. The villain's plan was to drop the cement on Mathew's head while he was waiting for Jack to let him into The Sanctuary. It would look like an unfortunate accident—a piece of architectural design crumbling off an ancient structure and landing uncannily on Mathew's head.

The plan had worked flawlessly to this point. It was 7:00 pm, and Mathew approached the entrance of The Sanctuary, where evil was waiting from the fourth-floor window. Mathew buzzed the number given to him and waited patiently.

Above him, the block was lined up as in the crosshairs of a riflescope. It dropped like a World War II fighter plane bomb. It plummeted toward Mathew and missed him narrowly.

With a thunderous boom, the block shattered, and the pieces scattered. Some chips hit Mathew in the legs. His heart echoed the exploding crash. He squinted up at the building and saw where the cement had separated from the wall. He considered himself fortunate to still be standing.

After a few minutes, however, no one had invited Mathew into The Sanctuary. He inquired and discovered that Jack LaRue had not contacted him about a meeting, and he discerned that this incident was no accident. It was a planned attempt to take his life.

The East Coast Intelligence Agency determined that the memo forwarded by Mathew's secretary had come from a call from a phone booth near The Sanctuary. Based on footage from surveillance cameras, they concluded that the perpetrator lived there. No visitor had entered the premises that day; the act must have been carried out by someone living in the building. Each occupant would undergo a thorough background check to determine if their past contained any violent acts.

Nicky Tomm was an interesting suspect from The Sanctuary. His past revealed a history of petty crime. He had many assault charges on his record and had spent a year in state prison, but he had now turned from crime to art—supposedly.

Ray Sota, an East Coast Intelligence Agency private investigator was sent to the neighborhood where Tomm had grown up to find out more about who he was. By canvassing the neighbors, he discovered an intriguing past. The Tomm boys, Nicky, Timmy, and Dana, had come in contact with the police at the early ages of ten, nine, and seven. They'd been caught stealing chocolate bars at the local Kroger grocery store. They'd been brought home to their father in the back of a police paddy wagon while the whole neighborhood watched in disbelief. Friends asked "Papa" if he was upset that his children had stolen.

He laughed. "I told them, 'If you steal, don't get caught.'"

Nicky had progressed to procuring and selling music albums from department stores. All one had to do was list the albums desired, and he would deliver them at half the retail price. He would just slip them under his jacket, and he was never caught. He then graduated to the more lucrative business of selling illegal drugs. At one point, he was busted for selling aspirins as LSD, which got him more jail time.

After his short stint in prison, Nicky had tried his hand at selling TV's—but not as a salesman. He would simply walk out of the store carrying the boxed TV without anyone questioning him. He boasted that he had the best guarantee in all of America. If your TV needed repairs, he would replace it with a new one free of charge.

Nicky was also a big fan of NASCAR racing. He spent a lot of his free time in his friend, Frankie Zimno's, garage, souping up street cars. This piece of information was the glue that connected him to Bobby's accident. However, without factual evidence to prove that Nicky Tomm had tampered with Bobby's brake fluid, it was decided to place Nicky under twenty-four seven surveillance, hoping he would tip the agency off regarding the next attempt at harming the Ryans.

Would this make Michael the next target? From day one, he had been very sympathetic and had treated the artists kindly—quite a departure from his father, who totally lacked compassion when it came to business. But the bottom line for the artists was to defend their turf at all costs.

Déjà Vu

Negotiations had been at a standstill for months, and Ron Henry couldn't motivate Michael to steer The Sanctuary discussions in the right direction. Eric decided to take matters into his own hands.

"Let me get right to the point, Michael. We need to accelerate these discussions with The Sanctuary. If we keep waiting, it'll cost our company millions of dollars in potential revenue." Eric slapped the spreadsheets on the desk and continued. "I've put you in charge of negotiations so you can prove to me that you have the ability to manage Ryan Industries when I retire. This is the first major project that you're in complete control of. In order to win the respect of our employees, you need to step up your game and play hardball with these people."

"Dad—"

"I'm done waiting around. If there's no progress in the next couple of weeks, I'll start calling in The Sanctuary's bank loans—as untidy as that would be." His chair groaned as he leaned forward, hands clasped on his desk.

"Dad, I appreciate you giving me this opportunity to demonstrate my ability. I won't disappoint you—or our company, and I'll speed up the process immediately."

Eric's concerned look lightened. "Son, I've groomed you for this position to carry on our family legacy, and I know you'll be successful. We'll touch base in a couple of weeks. Enjoy your day."

He believed, as Michael left the office, that his son would find a way to close the deal. Ever since Julie's death, Eric had coped with his grief by focusing his efforts on keeping Ryan Industries a world-renowned entity. This was his ultimate goal. Now to ensure that Michael followed in his footsteps . . .

Early on, Michael had realized that to win his father's approval, he had to become part of his dad's life. That meant being consumed with Ryan Industries. Since losing his mother, Michael desperately sought his father's acceptance. Whatever he accomplished within the company earned him his father's praise, so he continued his efforts to keep that praise coming.

After much thought, Michael emerged with a strategy to win Angie over by building a personal relationship with her. He would purchase one of her paintings, request that she deliver it in person to his office, and then diplomatically arrange a dinner to discuss the lighter side of the negotiations. He smacked his lips. That had to work.

The next morning, Michael found himself in Angie's art gallery, enthralled by what he observed. He hadn't expected her work to evoke such emotion. Her talent was exquisite. He walked along the display wall, then his heart skipped a beat, and he was stopped in his tracks. The painting of a field of flowers brought a surge of emotions. His mother had loved flowers—especially her daisies. Michael had had some life-changing discussions about flowers with George, their old gardener. This painting flooded his mind with those precious memories of his most cherished confidants.

"It's beautiful, isn't it?"

Michael turned and lowered his gaze to the short, senior woman in a black pant suit. "It reminds me of my mom."

She nodded then eyed Michael. "Oh! Are you Michael Ryan?"

"Yes, Ma'am."

"I thought I recognized you. I've seen your picture associated with Ryan Industries before." She lifted a hand toward the painting before them. "Your mother must have been a gentle woman that a painting of flowers would remind you of her."

He swallowed past the lump in his throat and turned back to the painting. “I’d like to buy this, please.”

“Of course.” She stepped up beside him. “Let’s go work out the details in my office. I’m Gloria.”

He shook her hand and followed her to the office.

After Michael had paid for the painting, Gloria asked, “When would you like to receive the artwork?”

“It would be wonderful to have Angie herself deliver the painting and decide on the best place in my office to display this masterpiece.”

Gloria lifted a brow.

“I’d be more than happy to pay for the additional service—whatever you deem fair.”

“Will tomorrow afternoon work for you, Mr. Ryan?”

He smiled. “Yes. Thank you, Gloria.”

She grinned back. “No, thank you. I’m sure Angie will be thrilled with this sale.”

When Michael got back to the office, he called for his secretary.

“Jean, clear off my calendar for tomorrow afternoon, and reserve a table for two during cocktail hour.”

“A business dinner?”

Michael grinned. “Maybe.”

She raised her brows. “A date, then?”

He shrugged. “At my favorite restaurant, please.”

Jean knew all about Michael’s activities and didn’t have to ask the name of the restaurant. She had attempted to retire last year, but Eric had insisted she keep working at Ryan Industries. Jean was too efficient to be replaced. She had been with the company from the beginning and had acquired a warehouse of knowledge over her years which none of the younger employees could match combined, saving the company hundreds of thousands of dollars. When Michael received his first assignment in the mail room during his high school years, she had educated him and widened his scope on running the company. Through the passing years, she had continued to mentor Michael up the corporate ladder of Ryan Industries.

When Jean had agreed to stay on, her one request was to work as Michael's personal secretary. Eric had jumped at the chance. She had clearly developed a soft spot for Michael after his mother's passing. Michael wasn't going to complain either.

Jean smirked. "You know, your mother and father fell in love under similar circumstances."

Michael looked away sheepishly. "Jean, this really is business."

"Mm-hm." She shook her head under the office light. "It's déjà vu," Jean said. "The Ryan strategy used to defeat their enemies is to make them their lovers."

"Jean!"

She turned and walked out of his office, calling over her shoulder in a sing-song voice, "It's true, though."

Warmth crawled up Michael's neck. He leaned back, resting his head against the high-backed chair, remembering his mom's stories and thinking of Angie.

It was true.

The next afternoon, Angie arrived at the Ryan Industries headquarters with her prized work and the installation staff.

She walked around his office, noting where the sunlight filtered through and how Michael's desk and guest chairs were placed. She found the perfect—and really, the only—spot above a loveseat against the far wall.

As the Sanctuary installer worked, she sat across from Michael and leaned forward. "Okay, Michael, what's up your sleeve? You didn't call me here to find the perfect location for the picture. There's only one wall that works. I may be a country girl, but I'm not naïve. So is it about the negotiations?"

Why did Michael blush so easily when Angie was involved? He felt like a boy who had just been caught with his hand in the cookie jar.

He looked Angie in the eyes. "You're right. At first I wanted you to come here so I could get to know you and find out why you're so . . ." He looked around the room, hands raised in front of him. ". . . so spirited about The Village." He swallowed. "But then I saw your work yesterday. It changed me. I was impressed with your skill, but more than that, your painting spoke to my heart. I could feel your passion in your art."

The small smile on Angie's lips drew his attention. He took a deep breath. "I really want to get to know you better and unearth what this country girl is all about before we try to come to some kind of compromise with our negotiations. I've got a dinner reservation at Union Square Café, and I would love to take you."

She didn't answer right away. Instead, she watched him as she contemplated the offer.

He needed to convince her. "Let me do this. Please. I promise, not a word about the foundry."

She turned her head and looked out the window. He'd give her to the count of ten before he resorted to begging.

At eight, she looked back at him, a soft smile gracing her face. "I'd like that."

Michael ordered a cab, and it met them in front of the building. When they arrived at the restaurant, they were seated next to a window overlooking a park.

After they'd ordered, they sat quietly, watching the sunset. Michael's heart leapt each time he glanced at Angie. *God, please give me the words to express myself . . . and the wisdom to know if I should stop.*

"Angie, have you ever listened to an old song on the radio that brought you right back to the first time you heard it?"

She nodded. "You can remember the exact place you were, and all the memories return to you like it was yesterday."

"Exactly." He tilted his head, peace filling him. "When I first laid eyes on your 'Beauty in a Cruel World,' the field of flowers brought back some stirring, impactful experiences in my life. He paused then, misty-eyed, continued. "I relived a time when I was eight years old, hiding out in the garden with George, our gardener. You opened up the door to my past, and I can't shake it."

Angie lifted her hand toward Michael and rested it on the table. An invitation? He'd take it. He laid his hand over hers, wrapping his fingers around her warmth.

"My mother loved all flowers—but especially daisies. Through George, both Mom and I drew near to God and discovered that only He could make sense out of our turbulent lives. Unfortunately for me, I've lost both Mom and George, my two best friends, and I only have my memories. Your painting evoked a flood of those memories. Thank you—for your artwork and the joy it brought to my day."

"Wow," Angie whispered. "That's the power and beauty of art. To be told that your work has brought someone joy is the greatest compliment any artist could ever receive." She squeezed his hand. "I'm so grateful for you sharing from your heart. Please, tell me more about your mom. You seem to hold her in such high regard."

He smiled. "Oh, I do. My mom, Julie, was the most gracious, loving, and kind person I've ever known. She made me feel important. She was a great listener and always followed up on my concerns with action. There wasn't a person in our family who didn't fight for time to spend with her. Unfortunately, I only had her for eight years. She died drowning. My whole life seemed to end there. I had no reason to go on living in such a sad world until Old George became my friend and shared how he'd helped Mom find meaning in Jesus. Then he did the same for me. Since then, my life has been full of purpose."

Angie opened her mouth, hesitated, then with a slight nod said, "It seems your mother was more into relationships than success. My parents were poor farmers, who raised me believing that God has a purpose for everyone and that our role is to find and fulfill it. They're very relational people, but poor. Money had nothing to do with success. Loving others and building them up was what really counted. I left my parents, whom I love immensely, to fulfill my calling in life to make this world a better place. God has given me a talent to paint, and through that gift, I've been able to start a new family—a family of artists who, in many ways, are searching for their own purpose in life. I hope I can direct them to Jesus by loving them in both their good and difficult circumstances."

The tinkling of silverware and the warmth of Angie's hand and voice filled Michael with a contentment he had never known.

She smiled at him. "I've befriended a young artist, named Mara, with unbelievable talent in sculpting. She's a flower who grew up in the cracks of the pavement, born without hands and yet doing what able people can't do. Her artwork is so emotional." Angie lifted her other hand and placed it on top of his. "I would love for you to meet her, Michael. Maybe it would help you understand why I've been fighting so hard to keep The Sanctuary. It's not for any personal agenda, but for my family."

They were quiet as the server refreshed their drinks and left. "You've made me think, Angie, and you're right. Mom was a people person. Money was irrelevant to her; it was Dad who tied money—rather than relationships—to success. I love my father, but he's quite different from Mom. I didn't realize it, but I've followed my father's path in life. I've always said I'm a relational, sensitive person like my mom, but I think deep down, I've believed that money is success."

"Michael, sometimes we're like that frog in the pot," Angie said. "As the heat is turned up, he's oblivious, and before he can realize the truth and save himself, it's too late. He's dead. I do think you're sensitive. I think you see the truth of your decisions and you aren't okay with the path you're on. Am I right?"

Michael lifted his drink with his other hand and sipped, taking a moment to think about Angie's question. *Do I want to change my path?* He nodded. "You're absolutely correct. I've become my dad, putting money before people. I understand why you've opposed us, not selling The Sanctuary, even for a huge profit. My mom would have agreed with you and would have encouraged me to reach out to those like Mara and help them become successful in life. It's not about whether or not I can make money off them."

Angie beamed. "I would have loved your mother."

Michael laughed. "You two are kindred spirits."

The server set their meals in front of them. After she left, Michael slid Angie's hand into his. "Do you mind if I pray?"

She shook her head, her long, dark hair swinging gently. "Not at all."

While they ate, Angie described some of Mara's sculptures.

"Sounds like she has incredible talent. I'd sure like to meet her." But in that moment, Michael's thoughts were fully engaged with the one sitting across the candlelit table. His heart raced. She was beautiful in both looks and spirit.

It was time to go for broke.

"I have to be totally honest with you, Angie. Today was originally about trying to win you over and close the deal for Ryan Industries. I've been so blind that I believed building a social relationship with you would win you to our side." His stomach dropped at the same time as her gaze did. *Please don't let it be too late, Lord.*

He set his fork down and placed his hand on the table, hoping she'd take it. He didn't know he had been holding his breath until she did. "Will you forgive me for my motives? I really do want to be more like my mom. And I promise you, I'm going to find a way for The Sanctuary to remain."

"Michael, it takes a strong person to admit he's been wrong. I believe humility is the most beautiful quality anyone can possess."

He waited with great anticipation tempered with a lingering trace of fear.

"How can I not forgive you?"

The weight was lifted from him, and he felt as though he could fly. "Thank you. Your strength of character and the warmth you've shown me by listening to my thoughts . . . You're an amazing woman with an unusually selfless heart. I really want to get to know you much better." He swallowed his nerves. "Would you let me take you on another date?" He ducked his head. "One not started out with an ulterior motive."

Angie's mouth formed an 'O'. "I . . . I think you're a special man, Michael—sensitive, in the good sense, which is rarely found in today's world." She tucked her lips between her teeth and leaned forward in her chair. "I would love to go on a 'real' date with you."

Michael squeezed Angie's hand, gently pulling her toward him. He sat forward and leaned over the table, drawn to the depth of emotion in her eyes. He lifted a hand, resting it against her cheek.

As he pulled closer, he whispered, "Would you mind . . ."

Before he could finish, she closed the distance, their lips meeting on a tender sigh that promised to fulfill every expectation. In that moment, Michael knew he had found his soulmate—someone his mother would approve of—and he was grateful to God for this remarkable woman.

Airmail from God

Michael tossed and turned in his bed, restless and unable to fall asleep. Thoughts of his mother erupted with smells and emotions while her voice echoed through the sterile hospital halls. He remembered her holding his seven-year-old hand and gently whispering in his ear, "Mommy is here." She had prayed breathlessly, as the doctors and nurses worked to save her son's life. Michael's mind raced back to the incident on that notable Indian summer's day, forever etched in his memory.

Their mom had gathered Michael and his brothers into the back seat of the limousine, squished into the compartment with pillows and blankets stacked to the roof. Being hidden amongst the bedding and picnic baskets made it difficult for her to snap a respectable picture. She giggled, and the laughter cascaded to the rest of the family. That was the photo that had prompted Julie to nickname the boys her little mouse, rabbit, and lion. Michael had sat quietly for the picture, while Mathew had bounced up and down, and little Bobby, being seated awkwardly, had roared with discomfort. After much reorganizing, they had finally departed for their lake house, affectionately named "Franklin."

After a full day of swimming, making sandcastles, and countless tire swings, the Ryan family had feasted on the world-famous hoagies and caramel corn of Mr. Jack, their household chef. They only got to enjoy these finger food meals during their visits to Franklin. The minute they started the lengthy, sad journey home, they longed to return. Michael knew now why his mom had loved these getaways. They were about memories, love, and a simple life away from busy schedules and suffocating business expectations.

Near their lake house, there had been an old country road. Michael recalled the day his mom had spotted the wild strawberries growing at the edge of the gravel road and had allowed them to pick and taste some. She had loved watching the silver birch trees glisten as the wind caused their leaves to dance, flashing their numerous shades of emerald. She would pause, soak in the beauty, and then sit her kids down to recount a story that her mom had told her.

It had been one of those occasions, and Julie had begun by addressing the big boys, "How did you two enjoy the strawberries?"

"Yummy!" Mathew had exclaimed.

Michael had added, "They're so sweet and tasty—better than the ones sold in the stores."

"Grandma once told me a story," their mom had said, "about a fox who tried to snatch some grapes hanging high on a vine. He was looking for a tasty meal, but he couldn't reach them. No matter how hard he tried or what tricks he used, he couldn't secure the grapes. After realizing he couldn't get this snack, he thought to himself, 'Those grapes are probably bitter. I didn't really want them, anyway.' Now, the moral of this story is that we often get bitter when we can't have something we want. Instead, we should be grateful for what we do have and not always desire more. If we want to be happy in life, we must be content with what we have and not fixated on what we lack."

Michael had always loved it when their Mom taught them lessons in the outdoors. These memories would trigger his mind to recall truths.

Later that evening, when the sun was sinking and casting amber hues over the earth, Julie had been towing Mathew and Bobby down the road in their wagon while Michael rode his bicycle alongside them. When they had reached the old abandoned race car track, he had asked his mom if he could bike around it. She had said he could as long as he returned directly.

Michael had mastered riding a bicycle all by himself, and he had wanted to impress his mom and brothers. He had ridden as fast as he could. He hadn't seen the old wire cord that had fallen across the track. His wheel had caught the wire and veered violently. He had been thrown into the air and slammed into the asphalt. He had lost consciousness after that, and he didn't remember the following hours.

Subsequently, Michael had been told that he had suffered a concussion and a broken jaw and that he had pavement scrapes all over his body and face. To make matters worse, he was allergic to a certain medication they had given him, convulsing with seizures. The doctors and nurses, after many frantic attempts, had finally been able to stabilize him.

For the next two days and nights, Michael's mom had never left his side. His blood pressure had begun to rise dangerously high. The team of physicians had tried everything they knew to correct it, but nothing would bring it down. Finally, the doctors had implored Julie to reach her son through a mother's love and calmness. She had gently leaned over Michael's failing body as machines and monitors rang in unison. In all the chaos, she had gotten on her knees and looked up at him with welling tears.

"Michael, Mommy's here," she had called softly. "Can you hear, Mommy? Squeeze my hand, Sweetheart. Mommy needs you to squeeze my hand." And to the doctors' bewilderment, the alarms stopped, and Michael came to.

Julie had had a way of making everyone in her world feel safe and loved. An infectious joy and a quiet strength had followed her wherever she went. Even a stranger could sense this. Michael's mom had stayed with him at the hospital for four days. She had slept little, saving her strength for lullabies and prayers. She had held his listless feet in her hands—the only part of his body not marred by the asphalt.

To lift Michael's spirits, Julie had had Mr. Terry, their limousine driver, bring vanilla milkshakes with bendy straws, and then she had sung him some of his favorite lyrics until he smiled and joined in.

As Michael replayed his mom's voice in his head, his thoughts chased other memories—a game of tag, for example, around the backyard bushes during a sun shower. His mother, he concluded was like sun showers. She brought out hope in every despairing circumstance. She was his best buddy, and she always showed him the silver lining—especially when there were rules to be obeyed which he resisted. Life without his mom was a life in which someone had turned the color dial to grey, yet decades couldn't erase his delightful memories of her.

Michael finally drifted into a deep sleep, but he soon found himself locked in a nightmare. His mother was lost at sea, warring the waves stirred up by a growing wind. The waters were a roaring enemy, and Julie was their prey. The sea had disoriented her, but she continued to swim, tired, frightened, and not sure which way the shore was. Panicking, she began calling for Eric.

In his dream, Michael called out to his mom, but she couldn't see or hear him. It felt all too real—as though he was witnessing the final, heart-wrenching moments before his mother's destruction. The dark waters grew calm, and he could only make out her silhouette. He heard a voice—

unmistakably hers—softly singing “Amazing Grace." Then she stopped, catching her breath for several moments. As she swam and drifted, her strength grew noticeably weaker.

Michael’s tears spewed out, rolling down his cheeks and onto his pillow. But he was stranded in a twilight space. He was half in reality and half in this dream world—an awful sleep paralysis—as he watched his mother losing her battle for her life. He tried to call out again, but no sound came. His pulse raced, and his soul agonized with each gentle wave that washed over her. His mother kept treading water while singing in soft sighs, "It is well with my soul."

Something glimmered in the opaque waters, and a silence came over Julie. She grew somewhat still. The faint bioluminescent ball glowed teal and purple. It trailed ripples behind it as it floated near her. She turned to swim away from it, but she was unable.

Suddenly, his sweet mother’s voice cried out in anguish. She dipped beneath the water then bobbed back up, breaking through the surface as though shattering a glass wall, and gasping for air. Something had struck or stung her.

Michael held his breath as tears continued to saturate his pillow. His mother was utterly losing against her enemy. Her tears mingled with the salt water. She mustered every ounce of strength and began to pray.

She spoke in a half whisper. "Jesus, reach his heart. Whatever is keeping Eric from You—please remove it. Keep my children safe, and one day, Lord, bring them all to me. I love You forever. Please, let Michael find my Bible."

Michael's mom began to float on her back, her face toward the night sky. She gazed at the thousands of stars in the heavens and started to shiver from the cool waters washing over her body. Her eyes were unblinking. Her breathing slowed, and her eyelids grew heavy. Julie's body cut through the waters one last time, never to be seen again.

A raven's cry pierced the silence in his bedroom. Michael's eyes flashed opened, and he tried to catch his breath. He found himself in a cold sweat as he sat up in bed. Moonlight streamed through the small space where the drapes were not fully closed and pooled on the floor. The burning sensation still stung his eyes, and he wiped away his last tears.

Michael was fixated on the contrast between the darkness that enveloped his room and the glimmering specks of moonlight. It was as though someone had taken tiny spoonfuls of shimmering mercury and sprinkled them onto the bedroom floor. He stared at the windowsill. There was the raven's shadow. The bird called out once more and then flew away. Michael reached for his bedside table and felt for his water glass. Slowly, clutching it with both hands, he lifted it to his mouth.

The raven brought memories from the Bible. The creature was found to inhabit places of chaos and destruction, scavenging on carrion, yet Jesus had used it to teach God's care, protection, and value for his followers. Michael pondered these thoughts. He sensed that the raven represented two alternatives. The kingdom of darkness desired him to succumb to evil, accept the status quo, and do nothing to upset Dad or the company's goals. His father would be content with another victory in the corporate world, yet he would be no closer to God than before Mom had died. Her prayer was to bring her husband into the kingdom of light. To work towards this goal, Michael would have to accept God's challenge and follow the way of courage. God had comforted Michael in his trials, and now Michael had the opportunity to comfort others with the same comfort that he had received from God. He could stand up for the Maras of this world, fight for their survival, and confront his father with his need for God to be his life—and the potential for him to be reunited with Julie in eternity.

It was decided. Tomorrow would be the day he would face his father. Lying back down, Michael continued to feel his mother's presence from the dream. Although he was anxious, he felt the Holy Spirit's strength as he pulled the duvet cover over his body and closed his eyes.

Operation Liberation

It was early in the evening, the optimal time to converse with Eric. Driven by determination, Michael climbed the grand, marble double staircase. The nearer he drew to his father's office, the more his emotions intensified. He felt a burning in his stomach. A dreadful despair tried to convince him that intervention was pointless. However, his purpose was unimpaired, and his footsteps forged onward, reverberating through the corridor and off the high ceiling. He reached the summit—the imposing closed doors of Eric's study. Pausing before opening them, he speculated that his father would be preoccupied with business calls but that eventually, during a lull between calls, he would grant Michael a few moments of his precious time.

As Michael had anticipated, his father waved his hand, motioning that he needed only a few more minutes for his call and that Michael should come in and sit down. He saluted his dad and chuckled to himself at his father's predictable ways.

Staring at the travertine stone floor as he walked to the far corner of the office, Michael noticed that no two tiles were alike, and he began calculating the cost of each step. He looked back, observing his father, seated behind his antique mahogany desk. It practically buried him in all its grandeur. The eighteen-foot ceiling felt particularly high today, and the sunlight fell more richly and more royally—more purely golden—through the office windows. Michael spun the globe that sat in the center of the library as he walked by. He listened to it spin, slow, and finally stop. He was about to reach for the library ladder, when his father paused from his call and offered him a glass of water.

"No thank you Dad," Michael responded anxiously. "Maybe later."

Eric gave a thumbs up. Michael, turning away from him again, kept his focus on the ladder. He hesitated, then headed to his favorite chair in his father's office. As he made his way, he gently grasped the ladder and pushed it down its track a few paces before releasing it.

Michael sat in the wingback velvet chair, tilted his head back, and closed his eyes, hoping to quiet his fears. He could still feel his mom's presence from last night's dream. Tracing his fingers over the steely blue velvet upholstery, he slowly reopened his eyes. He stared at the fabric on the chair, and he contemplated how the soft velvet resembled his dear mother, and the steely blue colour, his recent emotions against his father.

Michael was repulsed that his father, like the masses, defaulted to the same circular reasoning—that we live to make money, which will bring happiness. He had acquired exceedingly great wealth, recognition, and prestige, but he only grew colder, emptier, and more bitter.

A gloom washed over Michael. One day his father's zero hour would own his mortality. But then a deep warmth calmed him as his thoughts returned to his mother's passage from this life to the next. She had had something in her that Dad could never seem to grasp. Though it was left unspoken, everyone knew it. She had had faith like a child and a love that never left her—not even in her darkest nights. How could they be so different?

Michael stood and walked to his father's library shelves. He paused then lamented to himself. *If I could only flick his switch. I long for Dad to see not what he wants to see—a miniscule section of the painting of life and existence—but the entire painting with all its colors, shapes, and details. But his nearsightedness has blinded him.*

Eric finally ended his phone conversation and turned his attention to Michael.

"What's on your mind, Son?"

Michael's game plan was to alter Eric's thinking in regard to The Sanctuary negotiations while confronting him about his spiritual condition. "I want to thank you, Dad, for all you've accomplished for our family—giving us an incredible lifestyle with numerous opportunities to explore new challenges and goals. I value your confidence in me to manage a large part of Ryan Industries, and I appreciate what I've learned from you about how to be a successful businessman.

"I also treasure all that Mom taught me," Michael continued, "to make everyone feel important, to be a good listener, and to love others more than myself. But regrettably, I feel our family has drifted away from her ideals. She always placed people and relationships before financial goals. For Mom, success in life was more than making money. True prosperity was growing relationships not bank balances. She believed in the next life, and she wanted to live with that goal in mind. I want to honor Mom and make sure I'm doing the same.

"Just the other day, I purchased a painting from Angie, and it brought back so many beautiful memories of our garden and my time with Mom and George. My initial goal was to convince Angie that selling The Sanctuary and their other properties would be best for the artists, as we were offering them a lucrative deal. However, after spending much time with Angie, I discovered how much she's given to the artist community. She's a lot like Mom. She's compassionate, she doesn't have ulterior motives for personal gain . . . She has even reached out to a promising handicapped sculptress to give her a chance to share her gift with the world.

"I believe Ryan Industries could easily find another location for our foundry with all the benefits that The

Village offers us, and this move would create two favorable outcomes for our company. Firstly, it would give Ryan Industries valuable goodwill with the people of New York who dislike giant corporations that bully smaller entrepreneurs. Secondly, it would make the hiring process much easier. We want to attract long-term, quality workers, and these people are always looking for an employer they can trust.

"On the downside, we would lose sales revenue because of the delay. But we will be fulfilling a more important objective, the one for which we will be rewarded in heaven. The Bible says not to store up treasures on earth where thieves break in and steal, but to keep our treasure in heaven[1]. Isn't that the place where we all want to be?"

Eric began diplomatically addressing Michael's revelation. "Michael, I am glad that you have found God, but I'm not where you are or where Mom was, as I view the world a little differently."

Eric's words now turned harsh as he relived painful memories. "Where was God when Mom was out in the sea that night? Where was he when my brother was suffering—wasting away and then dying? I prayed so many nights for his healing, and God didn't answer. Crickets! So, I am happy for your enlightenment, but from my experiences, he doesn't exist."

Michael gently advocated for God. "Dad, I can understand your disappointment, but we live in a fallen

---

[1] Matthew 6:19-20 NIV

world because of sin, and to blame God for our trials is wrong. He sent His Son to die for our sins so that our relationship with Him could be restored. Mary had to watch her son, Jesus, be crucified. Surely her heart broke and she was saddened that God didn't intervene—but not bitter, because she knew God had a better plan. She trusted God, and Dad, you need to do the same even though you don't understand God's purposes.

"Last night, I had a dream that I believe was revealed to me by God. I saw Mom struggling in the waters, calling your name as she tried her best to make it back to shore. But when she was stung by something in the sea, she realized all hope was lost, and she asked God to change your heart and to reunite all of us, one day, in heaven. She also prayed that I would find her Bible. I thought about that all morning. We should have found it years ago, unless she hid it somewhere. I'm not sure why she would have hidden it, but if my dream is truly from God, then her Bible, I believe, would be somewhere buried amongst your books."

Eric rejected these thoughts. "It's not going to happen," he retorted angrily. "Ryan Industries is not moving its proposed foundry. I'm going to call in the bank loans and end this mess. You keep saying you care about family, but Ryan Industries is your family, and it seems to me that you want to toss it all away for a good-looking woman who has turned your head."

Michael, demoralized that Dad had rejected his advice and dream, urgently began removing books from the library wall, and discarding them on the floor.

Eric stammered, “What are doing Michael?” Rising from his desk, he stepped over the obstacles and made his way toward his son. Michael increased his speed, utterly dismantling his father's immaculate bookshelves.

As Eric reached his frantic son, Michael grabbed the library ladder that he hadn’t climbed since childhood. He scurried up to scan the top shelf.

“Where is it?”

Eric scolded Michael. "I don't have time to play games, Son. You won’t find any Bible."

Michael said something under his breath, then repeated it clearly. “You may not agree with what I have to say, but that's the point. You don't make time to contemplate your own life.”

Confused by his son’s comment, Eric interjected, "Of course, I have contemplated my own existence!"

Michael groaned, "Dad, not your existence—your death! You are one of wealthiest businessmen on the planet. When you see something you want, you conquer it, but you’re going to die one day. You’re playing Russian roulette with your afterlife."

Michael continued, "If you’re right, you will have nothing to gain. When that day comes, you’ll draw your last breath and cease to exist—game over! However, imagine the opposite! Imagine death is a doorway to one of two very different places with a threshold of no return. Allow your mind to go there. If Mother is right, you’ve wagered your own soul, and that would mean you have everything to lose for all of eternity. That is a bad business transaction—to wager something away that has eternal value."

Disgruntled, Eric then turned toward his desk. He looked at his watch and back toward Michael. "I'm sorry, Son. We can agree to disagree. I've got appointments. Are you finished making a mess?"

"That's the problem, Dad. You've never had time for anyone unless it involved making money."

Those words struck Eric painfully. For the first time, he realized, just how much animosity Michael had stored up against him.

Michael continued his search for the Bible. "Dad, do you see all the books on the floor? Half of them, you've never read! Life is like that; we are all indoctrinated or brainwashed. But know that there is only one truth, so choose wisely. You won't get a second chance."

Then the miracle occurred. To Michael's amazement, he stumbled across the book, which had been concealed on the very top shelf.

"Dad, it's here! I found it! It's confirmation that my dream was from God!"

It was his mother's small, worn out paperback Bible. Michael removed it from its place and, after stepping down from the ladder, began brushing the dust off it.

Eric was completely caught off guard. He had never given Michael's dream any credence that it originated from God, but how could he explain the facts? Eric recognized the golden cover. It was the Bible Julie had constantly read from. He also remembered getting annoyed with her. He had called it her "fiction book" once, and after that he had never seen her with it again. Now, twenty-two years later, Michael had uncovered it, hidden on the top shelf of his office library and enveloped with years of dust.

"Was experiencing suffering the real issue that turned you away from God?" Michael sincerely inquired.

Eric, still stunned by Michael's find, replied, "Yes, it made me realize that there couldn't be a loving God who was so cruel as to hurt good people. We are the only loving gods in this crazy world, and I try my best to help others out of their poverty and problems by giving them good jobs to support their families."

Michael countered Eric's argument. "There are no good people, only God is good[2], and that is why we all need a Savior if we want to spend eternity in heaven.

"Many people believe like you, Dad. They think that because there's suffering in our world, there couldn't be a loving Creator. They see death, decay, and suffering all around them and innately know something is very wrong—very broken. Sadly, the human race blamed the wrong 'something.'

"Job was handpicked by God for a specific suffering—not because he didn't have faith, but rather because he had great faith, love, and devotion. God, the Conductor, saw him worthy to suffer in His musical symphony. Why did Job suffer? Because it was a contest between good and evil, and God won. That game is still being played today. The

---

[2] Mark 10:18 NIV

world is watching, the enemy is watching, and—most importantly—God is watching. What are they all watching? They're watching us, like we watch movies. They're watching to see how each individual will react. What will each suffering produce in that human being's heart? Suffering is a seed that is watered through life and will grow into a mighty tree. But what fruit—if any—will it produce once it has grown? Will it bare poisonous or life-giving fruit? Will the human soul say—like Job's wife—'curse God and die!'[3]? Or will it say—like Job—'The Lord gave and the Lord has taken away; may the name of the Lord be praised!'[4]? Remember, Job didn't have the luxury of the book of Job. If you knew your suffering was not in vain, would it change things? All Job knew was his life was falling apart. He wanted to die, but he loved God at all costs and allowed the suffering to continue until God chose to remove it."

Eric stared out the towering windows. The sun was finally setting.

"Dad, why shouldn't we suffer?" Michael asked softly placing his hand on his father's shoulder. "Why not? If Jesus suffered so much—more than any of us can ever comprehend—why should we not endure suffering? You know Mother believed this."

Michael put his mother's Bible down on his father's desk. Something caught his eye—something stuck within the pages. He turned to that page and found the

---

3 Job 2:9 NIV
4 Job 1:21 NIV

photograph Mother had taken of him and his brothers the weekend of that summer lake house trip. Their faces were plastered with huge smiles because Mom had made them laugh as she always did.

Michael reached down and lifted it from the page as though it would disintegrate if not handled with utmost care. Then he noticed that his mother had circled a verse on the page where he had found the picture. He read it silently as his father remained unmoving, gazing out the window.

“I think Mom is trying to send you the same message,” Michael remarked. “She circled a verse on this page of her Bible, and this is what it says: ‘Blessed is the man who endures trial, for when he has stood the test he will receive the crown of life which God has promised to those who love him.’[5]”

Eric turned, and placed a hand on Michael’s shoulder, and smiled. “Well, you've given me a lot to think about, Son, but now I'm late for my meeting. Perhaps we can finish our talk another day.” And he proceeded to leave his office.

Michael watched his father close the door behind him. He sat in his father's chair, picked up his mother's Bible, and reopened it. Another picture spilled out. It was a negative from an old photo, and when he held it up to the light, it revealed his parents posing on their wedding day. A wildflower was pressed and stored between the same pages where he had found the negative. Mother had written

---

5 James 1:12 RSV

their wedding date next to 1 Peter 3:1[6] with three small hearts.

Michael closed her Bible and left it on his father's desk. Before leaving the office, he prayed a simple prayer. "Let my parents' marriage and all their shared memories bring the walls around Dad's heart crumbling to the ground."

6 "Likewise you wives, be submissive to your husbands, so that some, though they do not obey the word, may be won without a word by the behavior of their wives," (RSV)

Adrift in A Black Hole

Bobby lay sleeping, recovering from his second surgery, this time to correct the herniated disc. He had endured much pain from his broken ribs and herniated disc. However, the later had not responded to physical therapy or cortisone injections, and thus this second surgery had been scheduled.

Michael, deeply concerned for his brother, stared out the hospital window. It overlooked a city street that was relatively quiet at this hour with only distant lights blinking in the dark and the odd passerby. From this many floors above the ground, the cars in the parking lot appeared as children's toys. As Michael daydreamed, he pictured Bobby dangling out from a cliff's edge, well beyond everyone's reach. A clear metaphor—only Bobby could reach Bobby.

Even so, he had to try one last time to communicate truth to his brother.

While Michael waited for Bobby to awaken, he recalled the time he had first seen his baby brother in his mother's arms. She had smiled with her eyes and motioned for Michael to come and sit beside her. Michael had peered into the flowing, downy baby blanket, and sure enough, there was baby brother Bobby. He was so helpless, cradled in Mom's arms.

She had pulled Michael closer and smiled again. "Snug as a bug in a rug." She had used that phrase whenever she would wrap Michael up in towels after bathing.

Michael had smiled and requested, "Can I hold him?"

"Sit close and open your arms," Mom had replied, "and you can hold him."

Bobby had been a beautiful baby and had quickly developed his own personality—notably his strong-willed disposition. Julie would tell everyone of her feeding frustration, "I have to shove that bottle quickly into his mouth or he'll holler and scream and wake up the whole household."

Their housekeeper and nanny, sweet Heleana, had been run off her feet until Julie had discovered a secret baby hold to quiet Bobby. She called it the "football clutch," and it pacified him immediately.

Bobby's first word had been "no"—not "Mommy," "Daddy," or "Nanna," but "no." He knew—even as a baby—what he wanted, and he always did it regardless of consequences. One summer, as a toddler, he jumped into the deep end of their swimming pool. Mercifully, Heleana had been there to rescue him.

On another occasion during his toddler years, when he had been with Mommy in a department store, Bobby had wiggled his hand out of hers and run off, all giggles, as she shouted for him to come. She had hunted for Bobby amongst the clothing racks, crouching to the ground for an unobstructed view of the lower levels. Three racks to the right, her mischievous little boy had been squatting with his hands over his eyes in the hopes that if he couldn't see himself, then maybe Mom wouldn't be able to see him either. Unfortunately for Bobby, he was quickly corralled and confined to his bedroom for the rest of the afternoon.

After that incident, Julie had vowed to restrain Bobby with a baby harness whenever he was in public with the family. His joy-filled days of freedom had come to an end. Nevertheless, he continued in his self-willed ways, making life challenging for Julie. Although he was the most rebellious son, she continued to enjoy Bobby's affectionate side.

Michael kept replaying his mother's words about his baby brother. How could she have known how difficult Bobby would be? He was loved dearly, but he always pushed the envelope to unbelievable limits and left waves of broken hearts in his wake. Michael had tried, through the years, to encourage his brother not to waste his life on meaningless adventures but to make their parents proud by pursuing worthy goals. Bobby's destructive choices consistently led to chaos and a never-ending vacuum in his heart. The vacuum only increased, and the cost grew steeper. Michael often had to pick up the pieces of Bobby's poor choices, and he wondered how much longer he would have his brother. The thought of losing Bobby terrified him.

The vacuum in Bobby's heart was invisible and intangible, but it was more real than the physical world. As far as Michael was concerned, it took having your heart sawn in two by grief to understand how real it was. It took sleepless nights, a sabotaged appetite, and utter turmoil. And it took a good, long time. Then, when rest did come, life was never the same. But maybe that was the point. Maybe life wasn't about comfort.

All the memories of loss washed over Michael. He recalled how he had looked completely normal outwardly, but on the inside his mind had battled for stability. There were invisible walls that were only understood by the souls walking through those particular halls. So deep were the waters of grief that they could not be articulated adequately. "Hemorrhaging," was the only word that came to mind—especially in the early hours and days of delirium. The loss of a loved one was for life. You didn't come out alive; you carried with you that invisible missing part until it was your time to depart. These feelings and thoughts plummeted down on Michael as he remembered what it was like to lose Mother.

A gentle knock broke his inner scrutiny. Nurse Bye quietly smiled as she surveyed the environment and then proceeded to Bobby's bed with concern. She was elderly but full of compassion, joy, and energy that saturated every room she entered. She was forever optimistic and filled with encouraging words, no matter how bleak or stressful the situation. She reached over to hold Bobby's hand, and she squeezed it softly.

"Bobby, your brother is here to visit with you," she spoke in his ear with surety, "and your dad asked me to let him know when you'd awakened. He's down in the cafeteria, but he'll be up to see you shortly." As Bobby began to stir, Nurse Bye added, "I'm going to get you a new warm blanket. Your feet feel a little cool."

Bobby was a bit disoriented. Michael grabbed his hand and said, "Bobby, it's okay. Your brother is here. Your surgery on your herniated disc was successful."

Bobby started to acclimatize. His eyes began to focus, and he saw his brother with a troubled look on his face. Nurse Bye ascertained that Bobby's vital signs were all normal then left the two alone.

Michael stepped back and sat in his chair. "I don't understand all this, Bobby," he said with a sigh, "but I believe God's given you umpteen chances. I'm confident that Mom is with Jesus, and more than anything, she wanted all of us to know Him—especially you. She worried about you the most. Years ago, she told me, that one day you'd listen to me. I never believed that day would come, but today . . . I just can't process all this right now. Dad thinks I've lost it. But, you know, Mom left her Bible in the study, and I found it. I found it after a dream of her drowning and praying, there in that nightmare, for me to find her Bible. I'd forgotten how often she would read it, and that dream caused me to remember, so I started searching for it. God is trying to wake us all up," Michael exhorted.

Bobby sat up and held his breath. He looked at the cross on the wall. As he eased himself back down, he let out a long, deep sigh and asked, "Why me? Why am I still here?" Pausing, he thought a little longer then continued. "I mean, I'm not complaining; I just feel unworthy. You know the way I lived, and Mom . . . She should be here, not me . . ."

Bobby's eyes glazed over. Tears brimmed and started trickling down his cheeks. Michael moved closer to Bobby, placed a hand on his shoulder, and tenderly answered, "You know Mom prayed for you, Bobby, more than any of us. I don't know, but perhaps that has something to do with why you're still here. Maybe you should find out and stop trying to kill yourself. It's lonely in this family; you've got to stick around."

"I'm sorry, Michael. God is just not real in my life. I've tried it many times but without success. How do you hear God speak? He's never spoken to me or encouraged me to follow a certain path. He's always been silent. How can you love someone you know nothing about?"

Bobby turned his thoughts to his need to be loved. "Mother was my first love, and since her death, no woman that I've pursued has come close to fulfilling this void in my life. I doubt God could do any better. With Mom's passing and without her nurturing love, I've been lost. It's like I'm in a maze, seeking the way out, but every turn only produces a dead end. I feel like I'm falling fast into an endless black hole, and I might not be able to get out. You know what Albert Einstein said—that doing the same thing over and over, hoping for a different result is insanity? I feel like that's me, but which new direction could bring hope and peace?"

Michael sat back down to answer Bobby's plea. "God resides in a dimension which your natural senses can't grasp. It's only when you ask Jesus to take control of your life that you can access this spiritual dimension. The Holy Spirit then comes quietly and gently, not in the spectacular. Jesus came to earth unnoticed by most. They expected the Savior to be born in a royal palace, not in a manger amongst farm animals.

"There's a neat story in the Bible," Michael continued, "about a small voice that illustrates the Holy Spirit in us. Elijah was God's prophet, and he'd just called down fire from heaven, convincing the people of the true God. Elijah's enemies, the false prophets of Baal were then killed—all 450 of them. But the very next day, Queen Jezebel, enraged over the loss of her prophets, warned Elijah that his fate would be the same as theirs. Elijah was fearful, and he fled.

"After a day of being on the run in the desert, Elijah collapsed under a bush, wanting to die. An angel appeared to him, fed and nurtured him, and sent him on a long journey. On arriving at the specified mountain, Elijah found a cave and fell asleep. Later, the Lord woke Elijah and asked him what he was doing there. Elijah poured out his heart, lamenting about the people who'd abandoned

God, destroyed the places of worship, and now wanted to kill him—the last remaining prophet of God. God then ordered Elijah to stand outside the cave and He would pass by. At the mouth of the cave, Elijah saw a hurricane split rocks and then felt an earthquake shake the mountain. Next, a fire raged, but God was not in any of these mighty displays. Finally, Elijah heard a gentle whisper and realized that God was in the still, small voice. God then told Elijah to go back to where he'd come from, assigning him new tasks.

"The point of the story," Michael concluded, "is that Elijah's depression gave him a distorted view of reality. He'd forgotten that God was always with him and that He was greater than Jezebel, even when her voice drowned out His small whisper. When God asked Elijah what he was doing, the correct answer was that he was hiding—doing nothing for God.

"Bobby, are you hiding when God has given you a task to complete? You don't have to let the world's voice distort the reality of God. There are competing voices that speak to us constantly, by a telepathy of sorts. We hear them in our heads, but many people don't discern what's going on—that there are various authors of these thoughts. We have to be attentive to God's voice. He's speaking to us constantly, just as our hearts beat every second of our lives, but we don't hear them unless we make a conscious effort. Put on your stethoscope, Bobby. Shut out all the noise of the world, and you'll hear God. The more you read and understand the

Bible, the more you'll be able to distinguish His thoughts from the other voices."

"Do you hear God, every day?" Bobby asked inquisitively.

Michael thought for a moment about how to respond. "I don't hear an audible voice, but I have regular thoughts that I know are from the Holy Spirit. They're subtle. Sometimes, I have to meditate on this information—or sometimes it's the circumstances—to perceive what God is telling me. But it always lines up with His Word, and that's how I know it's from Him. Over time, you get better at discerning His voice."

Michael paused to reflect a moment, then resumed. "When I say God is subtle, I don't mean that He isn't powerful in changing people. Think of it like this. I look at myself in the mirror every morning, but I don't see much change from day to day. If I saw an old photograph of myself as a child, I would be amazed at how much I've changed. That's how God works. You don't notice changes from day to day, but looking back over the months and years, you realize that you've become a completely different person. You have different values and purposes, and you're totally unlike the person you used to be. But you have to be educated in God's Word to have the Holy Spirit change you. We talk to God in prayer, and He answers us—sometimes through people and circumstances but mainly through the Bible."

Just then, the door opened. Eric slipped in, and his sons greeted him. Michael, still feeling alienated from his dad because of their conflict over The Sanctuary, decided to allow him time alone with Bobby. He didn't want their disagreement to escalate in front of his little brother.

"I'm going to head out now," he said, "but I'll contact Mathew and let him know that Bobby's surgery went well, and he can come and visit."

With that, Michael gave Bobby a hug, told his dad he loved him, and departed.

The next days weighed heavy on Bobby as he tried to sort out why he was here and what this life was about. He began to heal physically, but spiritually he was more confused than ever. He searched for answers but came up empty. He concluded that if there was a God, that God would have to pursue him, because he was tired of chasing ghosts. He would take one day at a time and watch for any sign of a Deliverer who might rescue him from his spiritual prison.

Michael, on the other hand, felt a comfort he hadn't experienced since his days with George and his mother. He sensed that their lives were leading up to a major crossroad. Family dynamics were shifting like winds in a desert storm. Formerly, he had only hoped for such a day, but now he was confident that both Bobby and his father would come to see life differently.

Friendly Fire

Sylwia Trembinski was an enthusiastic, young reporter working for the New York Times. She had been assigned to covering the Ryan Industries-Sanctuary negotiations. Through persistent phone calls and inside contacts, she had procured an interview with Eric Ryan. Sylwia was aware that the negotiations were on the verge of a breaking point. What she didn't realize was that today would be the day. The explosive news from Ryan Industries would cause the dominos to fall.

Sitting in the Ryan Industries reception room as she waited to interview Eric Ryan, Sylwia scribbled thoughts nervously on her notepad to help guide her conversation. She had never interviewed someone of his stature, and she didn't want to give the appearance of a novice.

A voice disrupted the soft background music. "Miss Trembinski, Mr. Ryan will see you now." It was Sophie, Mr. Ryan's secretary, inviting her to proceed. She held open the door to Mr. Ryan's office. Sylwia stood to attention and strode through the door, holding out her hand to greet her interviewee.

"It's a privilege to meet you, Mr. Ryan. I am Sylwia Trembinski. Thank you for making time in your busy schedule to allow me an interview."

Eric had pre-calculated his response in hopes of a favorable spin to the interview. "I enjoy helping young and ambitious journalists climb the media ladder, and I hope this will be a big news story for you." Eric returned to his desk and motioned for Sylwia to take a seat on the black, leather sofa. "I've heard from one of our lawyers this morning that the Village artists have exceeded their line of credit and that the banks have begun to call in their loans. We, at Ryan Industries, are going to be moving forward with the negotiations to purchase The Sanctuary and the rest of The Village. We are willing to be more than fair with the group, ensuring that they are able to relocate to a more profitable location and secure their future."

Sylwia played the devil's advocate. "Your critics say that Ryan Industries has manufactured the artists' financial crisis. Many New Yorkers support them and do not believe that it is appropriate for large businesses to manipulate the banks according to their interests."

"We are going to provide fifteen thousand well-paying jobs," Eric countered, "and a large spin-off income for the

New York economy. If Ryan Industries cannot secure this large parcel of property, we may have to look at moving the foundry to another state, which would cost New Yorkers hundreds of millions in potential revenue."

Sylwia turned her attention to the violence aspect. "Mr. Ryan, are you concerned that the extreme Villagers may continue to attack your family?"

"We are coming closer to identifying the individuals who were involved in the previous attacks, and I can guarantee that they will be prosecuted to the limit of the law for their actions. Violent behavior will not stop Ryan Industries from doing what is best for our company. We are one of the most successful companies in the world, and it's not because we back down from challenging situations."

The next morning, Angie sipped her coffee in the kitchen and spread the New York Times paper on the table in front of her. The headline for the editor's choice caught her attention, and she dropped her mug in disbelief. "New Ryan Industries foundry to replace Sanctuary artists!" Eric Ryan, in an exclusive interview, was announcing the company's plan to break ground this spring and to build the largest metal casting foundry in the world. Angie gathered her purse and keys and headed for the door. She hesitated, eyeing the ceramic shards broken in the pool of coffee on the floor. Never mind that now; she would clean it when she got home.

Upon arriving at the ground floor, it seemed like everyone wanted to talk to Angie. More artists had gathered in the Sanctuary workplace than was typical for this early of the morning, and they all wanted to know one thing. What she was going to do about the news.

Pushing through the chaos to make herself heard, Angie's secretary advised her to contact each of her banks. The Village loans were being called in. She started with three of the banks carrying their smaller loans, asking for an extension. There responses were all the same. "I'm sorry, but we have no other option in this matter than to execute the order."

Angie's only hope now was to plead with their largest loan creditor, Goldman Sachs. Without an extension from them, The Sanctuary would be checkmated. Angie was optimistic. She had a good relationship with the manager, Greg Sanderson. She had come to know Greg from outside the business world through his wife, Jacqueline, who was a great supporter of the artists. Over the past few years, Jacqueline had acquired a number of Angie's paintings to fill their home.

"Greg, we are more than business partners," Angie started, "and as a friend, I ask you for the biggest favor one could ask a bank manager. Our group of artists is doing extremely well. There is little to no risk of us not being able to pay off our loan in the future. But every successful young business requires time to accumulate revenue to cover their start-up costs, and our location is a major reason for our success. We are planning a huge fundraising campaign, and

I believe it will be extremely successful, but we require a little more time to see it to fruition."

At this point, Greg jumped in and responded empathetically. "Angie, Jacqueline and I admire not only your compassion for the artists but also your wonderful creative talent. This has nothing to do with our friendship or the worth of your cause. It's very unfortunate, but my hands are tied. Eric Ryan warned all the bank managers that any of us who did not call in the loans would be targeted and that our careers in the banking industry would be over. We all know he has the power and resources to do it. If I extended your loan, I would most likely be replaced, and the new manager would call it in.

"Since your callable loans are not demand but term call option loans you will still have nine months to negotiate a settlement with Ryan Industries before the banks actually demand payment. But in the end, you will lose. There's no way around this situation. Money is power in the business world and Eric has it all. I'm sorry, Angie. If I can help you in some other way besides this one request, you know that I'm willing. Your friendship is important to both Jacqueline and me."

Angie hugged Greg and left the bank deflated. Then she turned her anger toward Michael. He had been given charge over the foundry project and property negotiations, and he was responsible for this new offensive move. He had disappointed her on so many levels, and she would let him know in no uncertain terms. She felt betrayed and used by him, and she couldn't believe that he had deceived her like this. She had been drawn like a moth to the flame by Michael's sensitive character only to realize that it had all been a sham to reach his financial goal. Angie had always believed she was intuitively gifted at sizing up people's motives. Now she was shaken by how utterly she had been beguiled by Michael.

Back at the New York Times, Sylwia's peers praised her for her breaking story. Her next concern was how to increase intrigue in follow-up reporting. Suddenly, she had an epiphany—a new angle to engage her readers emotionally and not just politically. She would go deeper than facts. She would explore what made these people unique. Family conflict always made the public hungry for more.

From her time with Eric, Sylwia perceived the situation to be more complex than a simple financial deal. But try as she might, she couldn't get Eric to open up about it.

Her next attempt would be to interview Michael Ryan and do a little fishing to find out what was going on at Ryan Industries in the family domain. For months, Michael had been the one running the negotiations. Now Eric had inserted himself rather abruptly and had gained the bankers' confidence to call in the loans. Earlier rumors had Michael Ryan and Angie Russio becoming more friendly and less rival negotiators.

After several unsuccessful attempts at connecting with Michael to obtain his perspective on the latest happenings, Sylwia's intuition told her that there was a cover-up at Ryan

Industries. No one from the company would tell her where he was and when he would be available for an interview. In the midst of her efforts to hunt Michael down, Sylwia jumped when the phone rang. She picked up the receiver and was surprised to hear the object of her search on the other end of the line.

"This is Michael Ryan, and I'd like to set straight the record on the negotiations."

Sylwia couldn't believe her good fortune. She rushed to meet Michael at a coffee shop in downtown Manhattan.

Sylwia's next posting was earth-shattering to the people of New York.

"In a dispute over the planned purchasing of the Village buildings, Michael Ryan, son of Eric Ryan, has resigned from the family's mega corporation, Ryan Industries. He claims that a conflict over social justice has caused an insurmountable divide between the company and his Christian values.

"'I have turned in my resignation to Ryan Industries as I could no longer, in good conscience, continue to suppress worthy expressions to our society in exchange for financial gains. I support the Village artists, their desire to work from a creative atmosphere, and their objective to provide opportunities for the less financially equipped talent. I believe both sides could reach their goals if there was a willingness to compromise. I would ask the public to demonstrate their support for these artists by donating to

The Sanctuary, which is presently trying to raise the funds to cover the mortgage loans that have been called in by the New York banking institutions.'"

Slywia commented on the interview then wrapped up the report with a philosophical quote from Michael. "'Wealth comes in many forms. You can be rich with regard to money in the bank but poor in so many other ways.'"

While most of New York was caught up in the family drama, a heart-broken Angie Russio had refused to pick up the paper. All she knew was that Ryan Industries had called in the loans and that Michael had been heading up the project. After grieving the deception she had fallen for, she was ready to give Michael a piece of her mind. She stormed into Ryan Industries and was met by Jean in the waiting area.

"So, you're the lady that Michael gave up his career for."

Angie was completely in the dark. "What are you talking about? I would like to see Michael immediately."

Jean answered coldly. "Well, you can't. He doesn't work here any longer. I guess you haven't read today's papers? He resigned in support of your Sanctuary, and now his father is no longer talking to him."

Angie was confused and overwhelmed. "Where can I find him? I need to ask him for his forgiveness. I believed he'd misled me, but now I realize that he is truly a genuine and caring person."

Jean scribbled an address on a piece of paper and handed it to Angie. "This is Michael's hotel and room number." Then she looked straight into Angie's eyes. "I've known Michael since he was a little boy, and he is the finest there is. You're a very lucky girl to have his affections. Don't hurt him. If this is about the negotiations, it's not worth it."

"I think I've found my soulmate," Angie responded, and she meant it from the depths of her heart. "Thank you for helping me and for your concern and love for Michael. I do sincerely love him."

Dark Gift Wrapping

The old saying, “When it rains, it pours,” was now most appropriate for Eric. In the past, it had never bothered him to be on different sides of an issue than Michael, but his exodus from the family had brought excruciating pain to his body.

Eric had, for some time, been dealing with severe discomfort, and he knew that harmful changes had developed with regard to his health. Still, he pressed on, not wanting his financial empire to suffer from his absence. He had hidden his internal pains from everyone, including the family’s private physician. Dr. Tang had hounded his patient constantly, pleading with Eric to allow him to conduct medical examinations. Now, because of his difficulty breathing, he could no longer make excuses, and thus he found himself lying on a hospital bed, waiting for his MRI test results.

The door opened slowly as Dr. Tang entered, a concerned look etched on his face. Eric sat up on the bed, prepared to do whatever was necessary to regain his health and continue leading his empire forward.

Dr. Tang locked eyes with Eric and began his medical debriefing. "Eric, I have some hard words to share with you. You have blood clots in your lungs, which is the cause of your pain and difficulty breathing. The reason for the blood clots is that cancer cells are thickening the blood by releasing substances that coagulate. The MRI results show that you have stage four cancer. Your cancer has metastasized into your lungs, lymph nodes, and liver." He drew his breath before delivering the final blow. "Unfortunately, medical science can do nothing to reverse your terminal condition."

Eric was thunderstruck—frozen in disbelief and unable to process what he had just heard. The thought that his life was soon to end had never crossed his mind. He wasn't prepared for this. He had too many outstanding projects.

After the most nightmarish moments, Eric snapped out of his trance, gathered his thoughts, and queried the physician.

"How long do I have, Dr. Tang?"

"We estimate six months. Undergoing chemo treatment would only give you a couple of extra weeks, and you'd have to contend with many side effects. Your quality of life would be better without the intervention. We can make you comfortable and help deal with the pain so you won't have to endure much suffering. We are going to give you blood thinners, which should help correct your blood clots in a few days. We are confident that you'll be able to go home soon and you'll have three or four months to function normally and get your house in order."

Eric, accepting the diagnosis, placed a hand on Dr. Tang's shoulder. "Just one favor," he asked softly. "Please do not let my family know of the seriousness of my condition. I need time to think things through."

"I understand completely," Dr. Tang responded compassionately. I believe that is a wise approach. If you have a spiritual confidant, I recommend that you discuss your diagnosis with that person so that you have good counsel on how to proceed."

Three days later, Eric was discharged from the hospital and returned home. He spent the next few days in the garden, celebrating memorable episodes of his life. One afternoon, gazing at the tomato plants in the garden, he recalled Julie's exuberant discovery of God's love, which he had brushed off as a silly phase. That morning, Julie had come bouncing into the room, holding a small paperback Bible, ecstatic that George had given her this gift. Bubbling over, she had wanted to relate to Eric her conversation with George.

George had pointed to the tomato plants and explained how people know so little—even about tomatoes. "Everyone calls them vegetables, but did you know that botanically, they're a fruit since they form from a flower and contain seeds?" Then he had asked Julie a question. "What does a plant need to grow and produce fruit?"

Julie had answered confidently. "Light and water."

"Yes," George had affirmed. "The sun supplies the energy for photosynthesis, converting it into sugar, while the water transports the food throughout the plant, allowing it to grow and produce fruit.

"These plants," he had continued, "which can't speak, are actually communicating to everyone who has ears to hear. Their tongue is not English or Italian; it's a heavenly language that can only be discerned by those who have turned on their spiritual senses. Just as light is energy for the plant, God's Word is food for our souls. The Bible is even referred to as a light that helps us walk without stumbling in the darkness. God's Word gives us understanding to make wise decisions.

"Now, water is a symbol of life, and it's linked to the Holy Spirit. The Holy Spirit not only gives us spiritual life when we ask Jesus to come into our hearts, but He helps us bear His fruit of love, peace, joy, and every other virtue that exists. Jesus is the only one able to quench man's thirst. We all have a God-shaped vacuum inside of us that we try to fill with alcohol, sex, pleasure, and the likes, when in reality, only He can change our chaotic lives into lives of peace and contentment."

If only Eric could take back those years. This conversation had made no sense to him at the time, and his lack of response had taken the wind out of Julie's sails. But now these thoughts compelled him to reassess his beliefs. Had Julie discovered the truth about this life? He missed her now more than ever, and he was extremely grateful for the beautiful gift of their three children that she had given him. They were a piece of her.

Then a horrible, wrenching realization overwhelmed Eric's being. It was as if God had entered the physical realm and struck him with a baseball bat. He didn't have three children—he had four. A flood of repentance overtook Eric, and he crumpled to his knees with harrowing groans. Oh! How clearly his great sin came into focus—his inhumane will toward his ill-shaped daughter! What kind of man had he become? He had placed his worldly identity before his helpless, innocent daughter. Not only had he rejected her, but he had tried to kill her.

The pain was too great for Eric to bear. "Oh, Jesus!" he bellowed. "I do believe You died on the cross to forgive sins. Please forgive my wretchedness! I am ashamed of all my heartless actions. I am responsible for Julie's death because of my pride in not wanting to live with a daughter who had partial forearms. Oh God, I have great sorrow for what I have done! I beg You to help me make things right with the few months I have left on earth."

A wondrous peace came over Eric. Language was unable to express it. His burden of guilt was lifted, and he sensed the love of God poured into his broken, melted heart. He felt as though he had jumped into the Mediterranean Sea, as he had many times in the past, only this time he resurfaced cleansed from the filth that he had collected from his evil lifestyle. All his selfish deeds and all his disgust toward the monster-being he had become left his presence, and a new hope of righting the wrongs took over his will. There was a fresh power of hope that afternoon—a changed, tender father emerging as a new creation with a heart of love given to him by Jesus. Eric set his mind to be vigilant in completing this final task. He would bring reconciliation to his family.

Julie's thoughts on the necessity of feeding on God's Word, still branded in his memory, moved Eric to his office, where he picked up Julie's Bible and began reading. For the next two weeks, he read and digested its contents.

After reading about Paul, the Apostle, Eric discovered that the old Saul and the old Eric had much in common. Saul had been passionately goal-oriented, hard-working, diligent, and focused. He had believed that followers of Christ were misled and guiding others down the path of destruction, so his task had been to track down these enemies and prevent them from deceiving the rest of the world. Eric was also passionately goal-oriented, driven, and focused, but his goal was the acquisition of money and power, and his enemy was anyone who stood in his way. In the present case, this was The Sanctuary.

Paul had been brought to his senses by Jesus in the form of a brilliant light that had knocked him off his horse and blinded him. Eric had had a similar encounter. His eyes had been opened by the realization that he had six months to live. He was in the midst of a paradigm shift, realizing how cruel his behavior toward others had been. Now he wanted to make everything right—with God, with his family, and with the artists.

During many of Eric's Bible readings, he would pause to converse transparently with God. "I have had a lot of bitterness in my heart because I felt that You ignored my prayers to save my brother, Daniel. I couldn't understand how a loving God would allow both Daniel and me to suffer—him physically and me emotionally. But after reading about Your crucifixion and how You were tortured for our sins, an innocent but willing victim, I began to question my right to be bitter toward You. But the final straw that shattered my callous core was what You said to Mary, Your mother, 'Woman, behold, your son!'[7] and then to Your disciple John, 'Behold, your mother!'[8]

"There You were experiencing horrendous pain, nailed to a cross, and Your concern was for Your mother's well-being and not Your own. That was truly unselfish love. What utterly convinced me to let go of my bitterness was Your awareness of Mary's emotional pain as she stood by You and watched helplessly, her righteous son in agony, hanging from a cross. If You allowed Your mother to anguish over You, then what right do I have to complain about my distress for my brother's suffering."

Over the course of his private two-week crusade, Eric also acknowledged how fortunate he had been to have had such a wonderful wife as Julie and how he failed to love her the way she had loved him. He had placed so much

---

[7] John 19:26 RSV
[8] John 19:27 RSV

emphasis on his business that he had forgotten how agreeable and selfless she had always been, even when she was wounded by his insensitive heart toward her feelings and desires. Oh, how she would have loved their little girl and made her feel valued! This would be his next mission—a long overdue gift that he wanted to give his wife—to let his daughter know that her mother loved her dearly.

Ruminating on the Fence

It was a wet, overcast day. A chill in the air gave retired Agent Woods all the excuse needed to remain indoors, catch up on reports, and whittle down a stack of mail. In his absence, the unfinished investigative reports and piles of bills had been left unattended. It was a reminder of how fortunate he had been to have a team during his days with the FBI.

On his desk was a collection of awards and framed photos of Special Agent Henry Woods. One of these—perhaps the most prominent—showcased him shaking hands with President Carter on the tarmac of Boeing Field. As the assistant to the Agent in Charge, he had been delegated to oversee the needs of the Secret Service while in Seattle. The trip had been presented to the press as a policy meeting with Washington State officials, but truthfully it had been a salmon fishing trip off the northwest coast at a private lodge. He lived large at the taxpayers' expense, catching chinook salmon in pristine ocean waters off the shore of the most magnificent coastal wilderness in the world.

Also framed on his desk was a photo of another noteworthy fishing trip—this one with his childhood friends, Brian and Eric. It had been an unforgettable adventure for a fourteen-year-old boy. The three had planned an overnight fishing trip into the woods by their rural homes. It was just as good a memory as meeting any U.S. President.

The ring of the phone seemed an intrusion of Henry's thoughts and an unwelcome interruption of the progress he was making. Reluctantly, he picked up the receiver and was greeted with a familiar voice. "Henry, Eric here."

Henry's mood brightened. He was instantly transported from the concerns of a professional investigator to his earlier, carefree life—a youth engaging with a long-time buddy. His friend, Eric, had always allowed Henry's charisma to dominate their activities, preferring to observe and learn. Henry had been the lady-charmer who would nonchalantly start a conversation with the prettiest girl in the room. Much of his confidence, however, came because his best friend was by his side.

"I'm in Seattle," Eric blurted out. "I need to see you. I flew in a few hours ago on the company plane, and I'm staying in the Elliott Bay Suite at the Four Seasons Hotel on Union Street. Can you make some time in your day to see me?"

"Sure, just let me move some appointments around." Henry wanted his friend to know his visit was important. "I'll meet you in the Goldfinch Tavern, off the lobby of your hotel in an hour. What do you need?" Henry had detected tension in Eric's voice.

"Can't get into it on the phone just now as it's complicated." Eric cut the call short with the excuse that he was being paged by a company employee.

An hour later, their meeting started off without questions and took on the tone of two long-missed friends reunited after many years. After ribbing each other over love lost, Eric offered, "Remember the night at the Empire Hotel? I was never more marveled by your charm."

It had been on a weekend when they were in college. The two of them had walked into a crowded bar, and Henry had observed a table of four good-looking, young women. Acting as though he knew them, he had walked over, pulled up a chair, and charmed his way into the group. All eyes had been on him as he had brought the group to laughter, recounting his brush with death when he had been chased from a field by a bull. His story was a complete fabrication, but Eric had said nothing as he sat down quietly on a chair Henry had dragged up alongside him without missing a beat in his storytelling.

Eric had enjoyed being Henry's friend. The two of them, without an entertaining invitation on a mundane Saturday night, had found themselves, in the company of four bright, young women, having a fun time. A bar server had come to the table, interrupting the moment, and asked the two young men what they would like to drink. Henry had looked at the large pitchers of beer on the table and had casually said, "Just two glasses, please."

The two laughed as they recalled that golden time. "And you never would have won Julie's heart if it hadn't been for my artful mentoring."

"Well, I need your help again, Henry," Eric began. The tone turned serious.

A great deal had happened since Henry had last spent meaningful time with Eric. He had devoted several days before and after Julie's funeral to helping Eric sort things with local authorities. But after that, their lives had drifted apart over time. They had spoken once a year to catch up on Henry's failures in love and Eric's pride in his sons. Henry's life had taken him to every corner of the country, accumulating adventures but with little financial reward, whereas Eric had continued on his path of monumental success in business. It was all in keeping with Henry's expectations.

Directing his thoughts back to the present issue, Eric began to debrief Henry. "I received some disturbing news. I have five months to live."

Henry was stunned, but he compartmentalized the news to maintain his composure. It was a coping mechanism he had come to rely on more and more as he grew older. "How can I help you, my friend?" Henry spoke with concern.

Eric stoically shared the facts regarding his terminal illness and his subsequent contemplations. Then he told of the revelation that he had received in his garden. Eric disclosed the hidden details of his most shameful secret regarding which his seared conscience had been revived. He admitted full responsibility for his actions, and after the humiliating specifics had been exposed, he finished with a plea. "I want you to find my daughter."

Henry sat stunned. This was not the Eric he knew and loved. The avalanche of shocking news was too overwhelming. He tried to gather his thoughts but could only respond, "I feel you blindsided me here." He abruptly stood up. "I am not sure I can help you. I have to think about this." No longer the bright, long-time friend, Henry looked stone-faced as he turned to leave.

"I will pay you $50,000 for any help you can give me," Eric concluded. He didn't want to take advantage of Henry.

Henry stopped for a moment, then turned back and spoke softly. "You don't understand, Eric. This isn't about the money. It's about a friendship I thought I had and a person I thought I knew and admired." Then he disappeared from the bar.

Eric spent the next two days working from the suite—taking calls and making calls. Then he visited an oncologist from

Seattle whom Dr. Tang had recommended. This turned out to hold no new hope; his diagnosis was just confirmed.

Eric understood that keeping so much from his longest friend had been a mistake, and now he was convinced that his confession had come at the cost of their friendship. He reminisced over some of the good memories they had shared. He chuckled as he remembered their immature phase, during which they had wanted to prove to each other who was stronger and more physically fit.

It had begun with a challenge to a wrist wrestling contest. Eric had become quite well known for having defeated all the neighborhood friends. To Henry's shock and disappointment, Eric had defeated him on more than one occasion. This had led to the evening in Eric's basement. When boredom had reached its climax. He had challenged Henry to an endurance competition. Eric had been certain that he could outdo Henry. The competition had been a simple exercise: extending their arms and retracting them back to the chest.

After ten minutes, Eric had begun to wonder if his challenge had been a wise idea after all. Henry, on the other hand, resorted to using mental warfare, saying that he could maintain this pace all night and stressing that he would not give in. After twenty minutes, Eric's arms had begun to tire, yet Henry insisted that this was the least taxing of all exercises and that he could continue indefinitely. Eric had shamefully succumbed to Henry's brainwashing and conceded him the victory. However, he had learned a valuable lesson that night. If he were going to battle anyone in the future, he would make certain to have the resources to continue until victory was secured. He had used this principle successfully throughout his career with Ryan Industries.

Eric's thoughts returned to the present, flashing on the screen of his mind a picture of Henry's disappointed look. "Oh Lord, should I have asked for forgiveness from Henry before sharing? I hadn't realized how much my secrecy would damage his trust. Jesus, I ask You to heal our friendship. I know Henry can find my daughter, and I trust Your promise to work this situation out for my good one way or another. You are faithful to Your Word."

The ringing of the phone ended Eric's conversation with God. Henry spoke briefly and directly. "Ok, I'll find out if she's alive, but I will be doing it for the memory of Julie and for the sake of the boys. I want you to wire me a $15,000 advance to cover the expenses, and what I don't spend, I'll be returning. Send what details you have to my office."

Eric was grateful that his distressed friend had not totally abandoned him, and he wrote down his account details before ending the call.

Putting down the phone from his end, Henry ruminated on his decision. "What am I getting involved with here? Eric has been dealing with a blackmailer all these years while continuing the masquerade of our friendship. What a jerk I've been for not seeing him for who he is. Julie would be alive today," Henry mused, "if Eric hadn't devised such an evil scheme. Even if I find their daughter, I doubt she would want to be reconciled to her monstrous father. But she should know that her mother had truly loved her."

Henry decided to go for a long walk. It was a practice that had proved, in the past, to slow him down and give him a clear perspective. As he headed for the park, it began to drizzle, but that didn't bother Henry. In fact, it seemed fitting in the light of what he had recently learned about his ex-buddy.

After trooping through much of the area, Henry finally stopped at a dinky diner to grab a bite. He ate his supper in solitude and continued to process Eric's confession. He recalled a valuable lesson his dad had taught him about difficult circumstances.

Henry had been ten at the time he had contracted chicken pox. He complained that the illness prevented him from going outside to play with his friends. To make matters worse, he had grappled with aches and pains, a fever, and all those ugly spots that had spread from his face to all over his body. When his dad, Hank, had heard that Henry was grumbling about having the virus, he had gone into Henry's room to cheer him up.

"Do you know what the expression, 'to be given a lemon' means?" Hank had asked.

Henry responded, "You mean when someone gives you a fruit that you can't eat?"

"Exactly," said Hank. "It's a useless gift—unless you squeeze out the juice and turn it into lemonade. Then you have something valuable and tasty. So whenever you receive a lemon in life, instead of complaining about how unlucky you are, try to make lemonade out of it."

Henry hadn't quite made the connection to the analogy, but his dad had gone on to explain that life was full of pleasant and troublesome experiences. The best way to endure a trial was to turn it into an opportunity. Henry had inquired how having chicken pox could be good.

Hank had answered with another question. "Is there a way you could accept having blisters?" to which Henry had responded with his own question.

"How can blisters ever be good?"

Hank, realizing he had Henry's full attention, had then challenged him. "What if I paid you a dime for every blister you acquired?"

"Wow, I could really get to enjoy having blisters!" Henry exclaimed in amazement.

That little lesson had had a huge impact on Henry developing an optimistic mindset, and he hoped that he might have the opportunity to influence Eric's daughter's sad story to conclude with a happy ending. Reconciliation between Eric and his daughter would be his desired lemonade.

Henry considered what he would first say when he located her. After much meditation, he decided the best approach would be a straightforward and honest presentation of the facts. If she decided she didn't want to see her father, he would not betray her confidence. However, he would try his best to help her see that reconciliation would ultimately be the best. This daughter had the right to know; what she did with the information was her choice.

A shallow person would feign forgiveness and reap the benefits of joining one of the wealthiest families in the world. But if her bitterness was too great to relinquish, then not even Eric's money would entice her.

Henry highly respected Julie as a loving and caring person, and he hoped that her daughter had inherited her disposition. If this were so, she would overcome the pain that Eric had caused and pursue the opportunity for a new life with her siblings.

Following the Crumbs

Finding a lead to Rebecca Porter was the easy part. Henry called his old FBI contacts in Georgia. No public source showed any record of a Rebecca Porter. However, an inquiry with the North American Registry of Midwives provided a lead. The last known address hadn't been confirmed in almost a decade, but it gave him a place to start.

Within forty-eight hours, Henry was on a flight from Seattle to Bradley International Airport in Connecticut. From there, he rented a car, drove to Bloomfield, and checked into a cheap motel. Old habits were hard to break.

There was a morning fog when Henry awoke early. He was just a few blocks from the Redstone Apartment, listed as Rebecca Porter's last known address. Standing at the top of the steps to the entrance, he looked through the collection of typed slips of paper stuffed into the intercom but didn't see a Porter. Her last known apartment, 3B was occupied by someone named Pipoli. This wasn't the person he was looking for, but they might know Rebecca Porter. He pressed the buzzer and waited.

"Who's there?" responded a strong, male, Italian-sounding voice.

Henry didn't answer. He held his hand over the microphone to prevent the street sounds from being heard. These old buildings were often equipped with unreliable intercoms. The occupant, not hearing any noise from the street, would assume it was broken and buzz him into the building—which was more than what he could hope for if he revealed his identity. It worked.

A knock on the apartment door produced a short, heavy Italian man in his later years. Henry opened his ID wallet and showed his Retired FBI Special Agent badge. He held it open long enough for the poor-sighted man to make out the large "FBI" but not the smaller-print "retired."

"We are looking for a woman named Rebecca Porter," Henry began, using "we" to imply that he was from the agency on official business. The fellow was convinced but said he didn't know Rebecca Porter. He had lived in the apartment for five years and had never heard of her. Neither did he know any nurses. Henry had him provide the name and contact information of his rental agency. The building apparently had no manager living on site.

When Henry returned to the building entrance, he paused, holding the door before it could lock behind him. Looking again at the slips of paper in the intercom, he noticed that one looked far more weathered and aged than the others. Apartment 2B was just below the apartment he had knocked on.

An elderly woman in a pink, hand-knitted sweater answered the door. Looking the part of a fit, well-dressed man on an important mission—along with the quick ID display trick—got him an invitation into her home. The room was furnished with antique tables and old knick-knacks—old but maintained in perfect condition, over the presumed decades since she had purchased them.

"How can I help the FBI?" she offered as she entered the kitchen. "I'll just make us some tea."

Mary-Anne Lanzel and her husband, John, had moved into the building fifty-three years ago. She had been widowed for eight years now. Without being asked, she recounted how John had gone to sleep in his recliner chair after dinner one night and never woken up—in the very recliner Henry was now sitting in. It had been John's favorite chair.

Henry, getting down to business, asked if she had known a tenant called Rebecca Porter, who may have lived in the apartment above her. She immediately corrected him. "You mean Rebecca Brenner from 3B. She moved in many years ago with her husband, Stan, and her little girl. The couple had their troubles with drinking and weren't the easiest people to accommodate. Stan had a cruel side. He always referred to Mara as 'Two-Thirds,' alluding to her missing hands and deformed forearms, and showed no kindness to her at all. He disappeared one day. Rebecca said he just left, and she offered no other explanation. I didn't press any further for a reason.

"Rebecca worked part-time at the nearby State Psychiatric Center. You would be surprised by how many women there become pregnant. Irregular hours and a child to cope with made her a stern and sometimes volatile mother. It's a small building, so it didn't take long for us to become better acquainted. Mara would wander down to our apartment when she was left at home alone. She was always welcome here, and she spent most of the time painting with the water paints John gave her for her birthday. It seemed to bring her some joy."

Henry looked up to notice some wonderful colored art on the walls. Not what he would have expected from a child, they were brightly colored shapes with a detailed depiction of light and shadow.

"The poor darling," Mary-Anne lamented, then proudly boasted, "Yet she didn't let her handicap hinder her artistic creations."

Mary-Anne didn't know where the mother and child had gone. "The two of them just moved out without a word. When Mara had not come down for a few days, I climbed the stairs to 3B only to hear from a neighbour in 3A that Rebecca and Mara had left with just a suitcase each. Rebecca had sometimes talked about moving to New York someday, if that would help."

"How old was Mara, Mrs. Lanzel?" Henry asked.

"She was about ten when we first met her. Her birthday was in July, the same month as John's." She paused, struggling to remember the date, which told Henry that she was genuine. Henry thanked Mrs. Lanzel for the tea and politely left her home. With the correct last name, Brenner, he drove to New York on a hunch.

Henry had a long-time colleague and friend working for the New York Police Department. He approached an unmarked, five-story, brick building in a light industry part of Long Island. To the right of the painted, steel door was a small doorbell. There was no indication from the street that this was the central office for the New York City Forensic Lab.

Henry having pressed the bell, a voice soon responded, "What can I do for you?"

Henry looked up into the camera aimed at him. "Is Rene Baily in his office?" He held his badge to the camera. "If so, can you tell him Henry Woods is here to see him?"

No answer came, but Henry didn't expect one.

After what seemed like several minutes, the door buzzed, and Henry slipped inside. Alone, he crossed the empty lobby, stepped into the elevator, and pressed the fourth-floor button. He had been to Rene's office before. As the elevator door opened, he was met with the sound of a nerve center of activity. More than a dozen cops—some uniformed and others in undercover clothing—were hustling about their individual tasks, oblivious to most others. It was in sharp contrast to the entrance.

"Hey, Henry! Long time since I saw you last." Detective Rene Baily was a tall, solid-built man, and he embraced Henry with a bear hug. It was a little uncomfortable for Henry. He laughed nervously, hugged Rene back, and then broke the hold.

Baily and Woods had worked together over ten years ago on a conspiracy case involving a bent Canadian lawyer and cocaine trafficking. It had come to an end when the lawyer had been convinced to drive down from Montreal to purchase two kilos of cocaine from an FBI agent posing as a biker. They had contrived a story of the biker's friend being in legal trouble north of the border. It had wrapped up with a currency seizure of $25,000 and a very unhappy ex-lawyer, jailed for fifteen years for conspiracy to traffic narcotics.

"Rene, I need some help finding a girl," Henry blurted out.

"Well, there is a recently divorced clerk in records. She's very into fitness, and she has a thing for older men."

"Very funny, Rene," Henry responded. "You know I mean someone I need to find for serious reasons." With that exchange, they had broken the ice and re-established their bond. Rene led Henry into his office where they could talk privately.

It was a good investment of time to meet Rene and half a dozen buddies at a local bar after work that day. He heard lots of cop stories and learned that Rene had gotten a divorce and married a girl he had started dating from the communications department. Etiquette prevented Henry from asking which had come first—the girlfriend or the divorce.

The background Rene had on Rebecca was interesting. She had some history of petty larceny. Her last known address was passed to him on the back of a New York Police Association business card. It held a dual purpose; if he were to be pulled over in New York State or any adjacent state, he could present the card for "special consideration." Henry had no intension of being stopped for speeding, so the information on Rebecca Brenner was more valuable.

The three-hour drive to Providence, Rhode Island, gave Henry time to consider his disappointment in Eric. How could he have keep such a secret from his closest friend? Could Henry believe anything Eric had ever told him?

With the help of his gas station map, Henry found the address and parked on the road. He walked up to the apartment. Years of weathering and neglect had turned it into a sad, rundown refuge. Walking into the lobby, he was greeted with a warm smile from a woman who appeared to be in her 70's. Looking frail but sounding stern, she asked if Henry was lost.

Flashing his badge, he explained, "I am led to believe Rebecca Brenner lives here."

"Not any longer. She passed away a couple of years ago." The woman stated the fact with indifference.

"Do you know where her daughter, Mara, located to?" Henry asked, eager to close in on his target.

"Well, she moved out about two years before Rebecca died, but I have no idea where she would be now. The woman shrugged her shoulders then continued to read her mail.

Now Henry's focus turned to tracking down Mara Porter. He called his friend Rene again to search their database for Mara Porter—or Mara Brenner—to find out if they had a home address or a work record that would clue him in to her whereabouts.

The following week, Henry was disappointed to hear that Rene had no further information on Mara Porter. But he had discovered that her name had been changed to Mara Brenner after Rebecca's marriage to Stan Brenner.

His search, now, was to locate Mara Brenner—not an easy task without a lead as to where she might be.

Two months passed without much progress, making Henry worry that he might not be able to achieve his goal before Eric died. Reports from the Ryan estate were that Eric's health was quickly deteriorating.

Then, to Henry's delight, he received a tip that an artist without hands was making a big noise in the sculpting world. He traced the lead to a resident at The Sanctuary, which was a large complex that housed many artists. He knew he had hit pay dirt when he unearthed the name of the sculptress: Mara Brenner.

Upon returning to New York, Henry called The Sanctuary and left a message for Mara, saying that he had some information concerning her biological dad and would contact her tomorrow to arrange a meeting. This gave Henry time to gather his thoughts. How would he inform Mara of the present situation? She was the forgotten, throwaway daughter who had become the Hope Diamond—the most precious gem in the artistic world.

Morning came quickly, but after his deliberations, Henry decided to change his game plan. Instead of setting up an appointment with Mara, he would just show up to avoid answering questions over the phone. He wanted to be face-to-face with Mara when he presented the truth.

Henry arrived shortly before noon, hoping that this would be a good time to catch Mara alone. The Village district was a unique place. The building-sized murals clearly marked the neighborhood as the home of some exceptionally talented artists. Over a short time, creatives from around the country had come to live here to display their talents, making it one of New York's most vibrant and trendy neighborhoods.

Upon reaching The Sanctuary, Henry took a deep breath and proceeded inside. The ground floor displayed the artists' workstations and prized creations, while the other floors contained their residences.

Henry was greeted by a large gallery with paintings by various artists and sculptures of wood, metal, and stone. A woman approached him, her arms plunged deep into the pockets of a long, knitted, grey coat worn over a white blouse and slacks.

"Are you Mara? My name is Henry Woods." He reached out his hand instinctively to shake hers, realizing too late that was a mistake.

She drew out her right hand and shook his. "No, I'm Angie Russio, the director here. Mara is one of our artists. She just stepped out for lunch.

"I have some important family information for Mara. Did she say where she's dining out?" Henry asked politely.

"You can find her at Benny's, on 6th Street. You can't miss it."

Henry thanked her and stepped back onto the street. He made his way to Benny's and immediately focused on a woman deep in thought. She was sitting alone at a table in the corner and seemed to have prosthetic limbs. Henry felt confident that this was Mara. He purchased a coffee at the counter and walked over to her table. "Mara?"

"Yes," she answered.

"My name is Henry Woods. I left a message for you yesterday. I'm a private investigator, and I was hired by your father. He's been looking for you. Can I sit?"

It was an awkward introduction, but Mara responded curiously and cautiously. "Please sit. I have a lot of questions for you." He was bound to tell her plenty of things that she already knew, but perhaps he would also tell her something enlightening.

The sound of the phone woke Henry from a restless sleep. Sitting up in his hotel bed, he reached for his cell phone.

A familiar voice spoke first. "Henry, have you made any progress? Can you tell me how it's going?"

Henry was brief and direct. He told Eric that he had found and talked to Mara in a coffee shop. For more than an hour, he had tried to answer her questions but with few explanations. Eric would have to reveal the truth. Henry told Eric what he had learned about his daughter. Mara had told Henry how cruel Rebecca had been as a mother. After her death, Mara had begun her search for her father.

"She's been looking for you, since. All she had was a photo in Rebecca's effects. It was a photo of Rebecca and a man named Mitchell, mentioned in a note on the back of the photo. They were standing in front of a New York medical building."

Eric knew who the man was: Dr. Mitchell Kelly. "Did she find him, this fellow in the picture?"

Henry informed Eric that Mara had tried unsuccessfully to locate him. Then he shared how her stepfather had abused her and how Rebecca had been a vicious drunk who had treated Mara as a prop in her larceny schemes. Mara's disability had brought the bullying of other children for most of her life. Only because of her art had she found a community who had accepted her for her talents and not for her circumstances. She was now a gifted sculptress, loved by the artist community.

"Will she see me?" Eric asked. "Will she come here so I can talk to her and ask her if she can forgive me?"

"I have arranged to pick her up later today and drive her to your home. We will be there in the late afternoon." With that final statement, Henry hung up. His work would soon be done, and he would have no reason to be part of Eric's life after this day.

Battle Lost, War Won

Mara had little control over her volatile feelings or the uneasiness of meeting with the man who had brought her into this world and then so cruelly rejected her. Eric had no idea how deeply he had hurt her. Being unaware of how much she already knew, would he try to downplay his guilt? Yet, like opposite poles of a magnet, she was strangely allured to meeting him. Maybe she was so used to abuse that she was drawn to it.

Mr. Woods had arranged to pick Mara up from The Sanctuary in the afternoon and drive her to the Ryan estate. There she would meet with her father, Eric, and her brothers, Michael, Mathew, and Bobby. The boys hadn't been given any information on the subject of the meeting, but they supposed Dad had some last words for them.

Bobby was still recovering from his car injuries, but he was well enough to attend without medical assistance.

The drive to the mansion was surreal for Mara. She didn't know how she would react or hide her intense, resentful feelings. This time last year, she wouldn't have cared. The car stopped at the side entrance. Eric no longer had sufficient strength to get out of bed, thus the meeting would take place in the inner master chamber.

After Mara had been welcomed by Mr. Stephens, the estate manager, he escorted her to Eric's room and guided her to a chair directly in front of her father, who lay in his bed. The boys sat across from Mara, intrigued by the mystery of the occasion.

Eric was in immense pain. He had refused the morning and afternoon doses of painkillers to remain coherent for this monumental talk with Mara.

"I am your father, Mara, and I ask your forgiveness for what I have done to you. I was such a proud person that when I discovered from Dr. Kelly that you would be born without hands and only partial forearms, I couldn't accept imperfection. I devised a plan to have you aborted—born stillborn without your mother knowing anything about my savage, cold-hearted plan. When Julie began premature labor, she was rushed to the hospital where the shocked Dr. Kelly delivered you. He had arranged with Nurse Porter, your stepmother, to plan for a secret adoption. She was hired for this scheme because she was without morals. However, she was smart enough to devise her own wicked plan to keep you, raise you as her own child, then blackmail one of the richest families in the world.

"When your mother was informed that you hadn't survived, she went into a deep depression. I took her on a long, Mediterranean vacation to help her through the grief of losing you. Julie truly loved you, and she would have been proud to nurture you, giving you even more love than your brothers to compensate for your handicap. But in my insensitive mind, I couldn't read the warning signs that Julie could not overcome her grief. One night, she swam out into the ocean, never to be found.

"I am responsible for the death of my dearly loved wife and for forcing you to live your hell that I deserve. But just as your mother had reached out to Jesus and found acceptance and comfort, I did the same thanks to God's wonderful grace and mercy.

"Mara, you need not forgive me for my sake, but I ask you to turn to Jesus—to let him take the pain that I've caused you and lift you above the evil of hate that fills all of us who live without God's life.

"I need to share one other important thought." Eric grasped for the hidden strength to deliver his final point. "Julie's love for flowers led her into a wonderful relationship with our now deceased, godly gardener, George. He taught your mom the love Jesus has for us all and his undeserved sufferings on our behalf.

"This was your mother's favorite Bible verse: 'he will not break a bruised reed or quench a smoldering wick, till he brings justice to victory;'[9] Your mom saw herself as that bruised reed after being raped at seven years old by a gang of druggies, yet Jesus poured His love into her heart. She recognized that He'd forgiven her of her sins when He carried them to the cross, so she likewise forgave her attackers and let go of bitterness and revenge. If you allow Him to, Jesus will pour his love into your heart and turn the injustice done to you into a victorious and powerful life."

Mara sat emotionless, trying to grasp her loving mother's insight and discerning her challenge to do as she had done by letting go of her hatred and bitterness toward Eric and her stepmother, Rebecca. No longer could Mara contain the pain and evil. Her soul erupted in anguished groans, like a swollen dam bursting apart. So deep was her heartache from her years of hurtful, agonizing pain that the room itself seemed to quake in horror.

Eric's sons, shocked by these revelations, were speechless. They hadn't realized that their sister was alive and had suffered a life of pain and callousness while being denied her rightful position in their family. It was a rare occurrence for them to act in such unison, but compassion filled their hearts for their sister as they stood and watched the scene unfold.

Eric, mustering all his energy, crawled out of his bed to hug his daughter with tears flowing down his cheeks. "I am so sorry. I am so sorry."

---

[9] Matthew 12:20 RSV

Michael, too, initiated a consoling gesture, trailed by his brothers, who gathered around Mara. Although Eric's embrace felt unnatural, she welcomed the strange sensation.

Still sobbing profusely, Mara was finally able to get out the words, "I need to tell the whole story! I am certainly wretched too." She pulled back and remorsefully continued, "For it was I who tried to get my revenge on you, Eric, by harming your boys.

"After my stepmother, Rebecca, died, I discovered a picture of her with a man called Mitchell, standing in front of a medical building. I hired a private detective, who discovered that Mitchell Kelly was a highly respected obstetrician-gynecologist and had a daughter, Sharon Wilde. This Sharon had followed in his physician footsteps and had become a general practitioner.

"The detective finally tracked the place where Dr. Wilde practiced medicine, and I took a taxi to her office to find out where her dad was living. I explained that my mother had recently passed away, leaving me with a handful of memories, one of which was an old photo. I showed it to Dr. Sharon and was pleased to hear that the man in the picture was indeed her dad. She informed me that her dad was living in the Manor Rest on 64th street. He was quite frail but could still get around on his own. I believed that Mitchell may have been my father, too, or that he at least knew the missing pieces of the puzzle that would solve my mystery.

"When I finally got to speak to Dr. Kelly, I explained, again, that my mother had recently died and I was ardently seeking the identity of my biological father, hoping that the photo I possessed would allow him to solve my quest. Dr. Kelly seemed quite confused, doubting that he could be of any service to me. But after staring at the picture, his countenance changed, and a startled, fearful disposition overtook him. He dropped his head into his hands and began to weep.

"Shocked at his reaction, I asked him what the matter was and if he was my father.

"Dr. Kelly was overcome with emotion for several minutes so that he couldn't speak. Finally, he composed himself. He told me that he couldn't carry this secret to his grave and had to confess it all. He told me that he'd been my father's personal physician. During my biological mother's pregnancy. My father, Eric Ryan, had had him contact Dr. Taylor of the University of Glasgow to fly to New York. Dr. Taylor had been the leading expert in the growing field of ultrasonic imaging. My mother, Julie, would have the privilege, to be one of the initial women tested, to determine the sex of her baby.

"My mother had been delighted to discover that she was pregnant with a baby girl. However, Dr. Taylor had later revealed to Dr. Kelly that I would be born with a congenital limb deficiency, having only partial forearms. Not wanting to upset my mother, Dr. Kelly had thought it wise to speak with my father." Mara hesitated and gestured at Eric with her chin, "to speak with him privately about this new development. He told me that my father, one of the richest men in the world, had not been able to accept that his child would be imperfect and that he'd therefore devised a plan to have me aborted.

"Dr. Kelly said he'd opposed the idea and told my father that he could never be part of such a diabolic scheme. For years, he'd directed all his energy to bringing life into this world, not causing death. However, my father had threatened to ruin his career and family if he refused. Knowing the power Eric Ryan wielded, he had no other choice than to participate in this horrendous act.

"Dr. Kelly said he'd given my mother drugs that would bring on an early abortion and leave me stillborn. Unfortunately for Eric, his hideous plan had failed. When my mother, Julie, was forced into labor, I was born alive. Dr. Kelly had arranged for Nurse Porter to take care of my adoption. He said that Rebecca was as evil as they came and had seen an opportunity to blackmail Eric. So she'd vanished from the district and raised me as her own child, receiving payments whenever her money ran out.

"Dr. Kelly told me about my mother's death. No one had been sure if she'd meant to commit suicide or if she'd swum out too far and hadn't been able to make it back to shore. But Eric had had the news spin the story into a tragic drowning.

"At that point, I couldn't believe what I was hearing. The only one in the entire world who'd ever loved me had died because of a lie. My father, who I'd desperately hoped still loved me, had tried to kill me. All the physical and emotional pain that I'd endured from Rebecca, now appeared trivial compared to this. I mourned for my birth mother, fantasizing about what life could have been with someone who actually loved me and then boiling over the bitter notion of a father who so hated the thought of his imperfect child that he would have me exterminated. I vowed that moment to take revenge on you," she confessed, looking at her father, "to pay you back for every hurt that I'd ever endured."

"So in my evil, after days of combing library newspapers on microfiche, I discovered enough about your sons to plan how I could harm them and inflict pain on you. I knew you, Bobby, were into racing cars and had many enemies, so I engaged with one of my fellow artists, Nicky Tomm, who had a lot of knowledge about racing cars, to tamper with the brake fluid. He was confident that we would never be discovered.

"With you, Mathew, I was already a resident of The Sanctuary, and one day I noticed that just outside one of the fourth-floor windows, the architecture was crumbling, and a piece was about to break off. I broke it the rest of the way and stored it until I could get you to come to the entrance, where I tried to drop it on your head.

"After that last despicable act, I realized I was becoming more like Rebecca. I hated myself and vowed to just move on and begin a new life, forgetting my revenge on Eric. Angie had been such a wonderful friend during this awful time, warming my heart toward Jesus.

"I am sincerely ashamed of my actions, and I'm willing to face their consequences. I've been no better than you, Dad. But you're right—only Jesus can change our sinful natures. I forgive you from my heart, Dad, and I ask the forgiveness of you and my brothers."

Bobby and Mathew gathered around Mara to hug her.

"Sis, you put sense in my head," Bobby commented, "and I'm grateful for the time I spent in the hospital. It made me realize that I no longer wanted to pursue my selfish lifestyle."

"I didn't get hurt," Mathew added, "and I know how much you've suffered. Let's just move on from here."

Dad turned to Mara and said, "God has answered my most precious prayer. He has reconciled me to my daughter whom I foolishly abandoned. In honor of you, Mara, I want to pay off all the loans for The Sanctuary and let you have an opportunity to use your gift of sculpting for the world to enjoy."

Michael hugged his father. "Thank you, Dad," he whispered. "You're my hero."

Demystifying the Puzzle

Three days later, Eric passed away peacefully with his family at his side. Mara's head rested affectionately on his chest, making up for the love that had been squandered away because of evil.

Michael had asked Angie to marry him, and she had jubilantly accepted. He had surpassed all her expectations for what kind of person her future husband would be. Her knight in shining armor had defended her love for her fellow artists at the risk of losing everything he treasured—even his relationship with his dad. But God had been gracious to the entire family and had answered Michael's prayer, bringing reconciliation throughout the family.

In the midst of the revelations of the past few days, Angie and Mara had grown extremely close, and now they would become related through Angie's marriage to Michael. However, even if they had been born sisters, their true connection was now greater still because they were joined by the blood of Christ. They found it to be a much stronger and more enduring bond than any marriage contract or birth relationship could bring.

Michael was in awe of God's supernatural intervention, and he questioned why he had received such favor. First, God had brought Angie into his life. Then He had given him a dream that confirmed that his mother's death hadn't been suicide but God's will in calling her home.

The Lord had also revealed his mother's final prayer, allowing Michael to discover her lost Bible, which had compelled him to challenge his dad to turn to Jesus. To press the issue, God had created a short window of time for Eric by revealing his advanced cancer that would soon end his life. Eric's soul searching had led to the Holy Spirit's exposure of his greatest regret, the rejection of his daughter, to which he had responded by repenting and turning to the grace of God to help him right his wrongs.

Finally, God had allowed Mara, who had endured a life of hate and pain, to release her bitterness and experience the unconditional love of their heavenly Father. Life could not get any better than this—from a young boy mourning the loss of his endeared mother to the reconciliation of their family to the exciting expectation of raising his own children and the future hope of being united, one day, with his beloved mother and father in eternity.

The morning before Eric's memorial, Michael sat in his father's study and began reading the creation account in the Bible. He read that on day six God had created crawling creatures, domesticated animals, and wild animals, and that man's task had been to represent God and rule over all His creation. Adam had even gotten the opportunity to name all the animals.

After meditating on the three kinds of animals, a thought struck Michael. He had the fortune to associate these groups of animals with spiritual classes—classes that appeared to represent his three siblings.

Mara had, in a sense, survived life as a wild animal, having been treated as less than human by her stepparents. She had been physically and mentally abused, rejected by her biological father, and less valued by much of society. She had had to fend for herself, living in her wilderness, and it was little wonder that she hadn't responded to her conscience when she had tried to harm Bobby and Mathew. That inner voice had become seared from the trauma she had suffered.

Bobby seemed to fit into the group of crawling creatures—specifically a caterpillar, which lived an earthy life, crawling in the mud and having only the fleshly desires of devouring as many leaves as possible. Presently, he was battling the need to turn to Jesus—to be metamorphosized into a butterfly that could soar in the atmosphere and experience the real splendors of life.

The domesticated animal truly symbolized Mathew. These animals' purpose in life was usefulness—to benefit their master by completing his tasks—and they were faithful and reliable in these services. However, these animals didn't enjoy the intimacy of a relationship with their master. They seemed accepting of their position in life and content in receiving their daily food, not desiring more than what they were experiencing. Mathew was content in knowing there was a God and respecting Him, but he had little interest in pursuing an intimate relationship with the Creator of the universe.

Now Michael considered his calling. God had accepted him as His child, and Michael's role was to be God's ambassador—to open windows and unlock doors for the three groups of imprisoned animals. Let them be unshackled and enjoy true freedom! God wanted everyone, regardless of their past or present circumstances, to live a life above the clouds—to soar as an eagle in the heavenlies rather than to subsist and be ground-bound.

Michael would devote his energies to fulfilling his calling by encouraging his siblings, Angie, and everyone whom he befriended, so that they could discover and enjoy their life's purpose.

Eric's memorial was held in the garden on a beautiful, sunny day. Michael, standing beside Julie's favorite statue, "A Mother and Her Baby," turned to Mara and said, "You are Julie's cherished flower, Mara."

Mara responded with sobbing tears. Michael had been so gracious in welcoming her into the family as their beloved sister, despite her attempts to harm her siblings. "I've felt worthless all my life. It is incredibly difficult to see myself, now, as one of Julie's treasured flowers."

Angie and Michael embraced Mara. They wanted her to know that she was not only accepted but loved by all her family.

Michael then announced to everyone in the garden, "I need to share something very special: the message that I left for Mom in my favorite tin box at her memorial. It's a message I believe God has answered this very day—one that is as amazing as all the miracles that He has done in the past few months—and I believe it was because of Mom's prayers for all of us."

Michael laid trembling hands on that weathered tin box, fingers poised to open it after all these years . . .

To hear Michael's message, go to
http://morningdevotions.se/jf

Hidden Manna

For all who enjoyed exercising their sleuthing skills by fitting together the story's puzzle pieces, I have included this bonus chapter for you to uncover more hidden treasure. This investigation is for the astute—those who have insight and exceptional discernment.

The answers are found after the questions.

Question One:

Private Investigator Gary Goveno once said that to solve a complex mystery, in metaphorical terms, is the difference between gathering tomatoes and potatoes. What did he mean?

Question Two:

Discern the symbolic meaning of the *Julie's Flowers* logo featured in the image at the beginning of this chapter.

Question Three:

Discern the symbolic meaning of the *Streeter and Tang* logo featured in the image at the beginning of this chapter.

Question Four:

What is God's 2:1 principle for winning friends, found in the first chapter of the book of James?

Question Five:

Tang wrote the lyric, "Life is all about lost and found." In light of this novel, can you deduce the meaning of the lyric?

Answer to Question One:

Tomatoes are easy to gather as they grow above the ground. Potatoes, on the other hand, require additional labor—digging beneath the surface. To solve a difficult mystery, the sleuth must be prepared to dig for the hidden clues rather than gather only observable evidence.

To discover the deep truths of God, one must carefully observe and diligently study the Bible.

Answer to Question Two:

The three yellow daisies represent Eric and Julie's three sons, Michael, Mathew, and Bobby. The white daisy depicts their daughter Mara. The stems symbolize Eric and Julie's hands holding their children up by nurturing them with love and guidance. Unfortunately, Mara didn't receive parental support as a child.

Flowers are also a blessing to everyone; they are pretty to look at and dispense a pleasant aroma. Julie's flowers turned out to be a blessing by their good deeds and encouraging words to others.

We are to be a pleasant aroma to those around us.

> *But thanks be to God, who always leads us as captives in Christ's triumphal procession and uses us to spread the* ***aroma of the knowledge of him*** *everywhere. For we are to God the pleasing aroma of Christ among those who are being saved and those who are perishing. To the one we are an aroma that brings death; to the other,* ***an aroma that brings life****[...]*
> *-2 Corinthians 2:14-16 (NIV), bold formatting added by me*

Answer to Question Three:

The three "t's" symbolize the three crosses at Calvary where Jesus was crucified to pay for our sins. The first cross is white, portraying Jesus as the sinless lamb who took away the sin of the world.

The next day John saw Jesus coming toward him and said, "Look, the ***Lamb of God****, who* ***takes away*** *the* ***sin*** *of the world!*
–John 1:29 (NIV), bold formatting added by me

The "s" twisted around the first "t" represents Moses' bronze snake on a pole, which healed anyone who had been bitten by a venomous snake if they looked at it.

So Moses made a bronze snake and put it up on a pole. Then when anyone was bitten by a snake and ***looked*** *at the bronze snake, they* ***lived****.*
–Numbers 21:9 (NIV), bold formatting added by me

Jesus' death paid for our sins, but we must trust in this truth by becoming dependent upon Christ to receive eternal life.

Just as Moses lifted up the snake in the wilderness, so the Son of Man must be lifted up, that everyone who ***believes*** *may have* ***eternal life*** *in him.*
–John 3:14-15 (NIV), bold formatting added by me

I have been crucified with Christ and I no longer live, but Christ lives in me. The life I now live in the body, ***I live by faith in the Son of God****, who loved me and gave himself for me.*
–Galatians 2:20, bold formatting added by me

The black second and third crosses represent Streeter and Tang, born sinners.

*As for you, you were **dead in** your transgressions and **sins**, in which you used to live when you followed the ways of this world and of the ruler of the kingdom of the air, the spirit who is now at work in those who are disobedient. All of us also lived among them at one time, gratifying the cravings of our flesh and following its desires and thoughts. Like the rest, we were by nature deserving of wrath.*
–Ephesians 2:1-3 (NIV), bold formatting added by me

These black crosses have now turned white because we have turned to receive Jesus' gift of righteousness, which is one of the many blessings included in the gift of eternal life.

*For God so loved the world that he gave his one and only Son, that whoever **believes in him** shall not perish but have **eternal life**.*
–John 3:16, bold formatting added by me

*God made him who had no sin to be sin for us, so that in him we might become the **righteousness of God**.*
–2 Corinthians 5:21 (NIV), bold formatting added by me

The three "t's" also embody the truth that Jesus, husband, and wife make a strong bond which brings victory.

Though one may be overpowered, two can defend themselves. A cord of ***three strands*** *is not quickly broken.*
–Ecclesiastes 4:12 (NIV), bold formatting added by me

Answer to Question Four:

God gave us two ears but only one mouth to remind us to listen twice as much as we speak. James 1:19 states, "Be quick to listen, slow to speak and slow to become angry." When we are active listeners, able to rephrase what our speaker has shared, he or she will value us as a good friend because we have honored him or her by listening intently to his or her thoughts. Everyone wants to be heard; it's a basic need we all have. If we are good and active listeners, we will have many friends.

The third command to be slow to anger concerns our minds.

The cerebral cortex (cortex) is the thinking part of the brain where logic and judgment reside. It is the outer portion of the brain and is divided into lobes. [...]
The emotional center of the brain is the limbic system. It is located lower in the brain and is considered to be more primitive than the cortex.
When someone is experiencing and expressing anger, he or she is not using the thinking (cortex) part of the brain, but primarily, the limbic center of the brain.

–How Does Anger Happen in the Brain, LakesideLink.com

God reminds us to use the cortex part when responding to others to avoid angry retaliations.

Answer to Question Five:

Eric and Julie both had traumatic experiences as children. Julie was raped at age seven. Eric, at nine, was responsible for his brother's accident and eventual death. They were guileless children, but because of their ordeals, they alienated themselves from others and became lonely. They kept their respective secrets within themselves and suffered the consequences. Julie grew up believing she had little worth as a person, and Eric buried his fateful memories beneath activity and striving for success.

They were two lost souls, but God wasn't going to leave them in that condition. He used George, the gardener, to speak to Julie about the worth she had in His eyes, and she responded by turning her life to loving her Savior. She not only found the One who truly loved her, but she discovered how to love others.

Eric, on the other hand, was a harder nut to crack. God allowed him to reach the end of his rope before he would look upward. God exposed Eric's evil actions toward his daughter after the knowledge of his imminent death, capturing his attention to address his sin and creating in him a passion to make things right. He couldn't change what had happened to his brother, but he could stop blaming God and take responsibility for his actions. The result of his repentance was peace and joy with the objective of reconciling his family to God. Eric let go of his bitterness and hate, and he found the love of God—the reason each of us exist today.

God's grace was also sufficient to heal Mara's wounds, and it's ample to heal yours.

"When the world has used you up
And its lies have left you broken,
Oh, His love can heal your wounds
And His Word you can trust in."
–His Love Can Conquer Mountains, Streeter and Tang.

There is one important life decision, which is to recognize your lost condition—your separation from the righteous Creator. If you choose to be found by believing in the gospel, it will result in an eternity with God where there is no longer any death, mourning, tears, or pain, but rather it is filled with love, meaning, and purpose.

If this is your desire, type the following hyperlink into your browser to find out how to be saved:

http://morningdevotions.se/

Note from the Author

Nearly thirty-five years ago, Tang received a full-length, cinematic dream and shared it with her family and friends. It was such an imaginative vision that many encouraged her to turn it into a novel. In 2015, she began the process of fashioning her dream into a book.

Unfortunately for Streeter, Tang entered an eight-month battle with cancer, ending with her promotion to heaven. Without his soulmate, Streeter struggled to fill his loneliness with whatever he could. Then he thought to honor his best friend by completing her half-finished novel. This project gave him significant purpose. With the help of several good friends and family members, Tang's novel has come to life.

Tang was the first to uncover the priceless treasure of worthwhile purpose, and then she passed it on to Streeter and many others. Their book offers insight on this gnaw that everyone feels, yet many are bewildered about where to find its solution. Learn this valuable truth as you eavesdrop in on the Ryan clan who—in all their affluence—are unable to fill their void. How strange the events that finally opened their eyes!

Acknowledgements

I, Streeter, would like to thank the following people for making this novel possible:

Tang for the intriguing plot. Originally, she had titled the book Laura's Flowers after our niece, who lived with us for a little while, but when I recognized that the character she was writing was a replica of herself, I changed the title to Julie's Flowers, "Julie" being Tang's real name.

Julia Danielsson, our eldest daughter, who helped write chapter 10, "Opposites Attract."

Rachael Strean, our middle child, who wrote chapters 13 and 14, "Air Mail from God" and "Operation Liberation."

Megan Elizabeth Saxton who designed the book's front cover.

Henry Widdows, Tang's brother and my best friend, who wrote chapters 18 and 19, "Ruminating on the Fence" and "Following the Crumbs."

Mikal Dawn, our daughter Julia's good friend, who wrote chapter 12, "Déjà Vu."

Evan Mejia who sketched the chapter illustrations.

Jordy Leigh, whom I discovered by accident by reading her blog and realized that she had immense talent. I asked her to edit our novel and bring coherence to the story—a difficult task for anyone given that it had six different writers. She not only did a brilliant job editing but helped extensively with chapters 8 and 16, “Zoning In” and “Friendly Fire.” She also wrote the blurb for the back cover.

Author Bio

Streeter and Tang are the pen names of george and Julia Farkas. Years ago, george swapped his capital "G" for a lower case "g" to remind him that pride, left unbridled, has the power to destroy his most cherished relationships. Julia was known as "Julie" because george mistakenly believed it was the short form of her name, as "Sophie" is the diminutive version of "Sophia." It wasn't until ten years into their marriage that Julia informed george that her real name wasn't "Julie." She said she hadn't wanted to correct him since he seemed enthralled by the exciting thoughts conjured up by the name "Julie."

The couple's first published book was an autobiography called *If God Gave Me A Voice*. It described the many miracles that they had experienced in both good and challenging times with regard to jobs, houses, friends, and finances. Behind every victory was the goodness and faithfulness of God.

This latest book was begun by Tang and completed with a little help from her friends. In 1976, she painted a picture of a field of daisies, which her sister-in-law purchased as a Mother's Day gift. Years later, when her sister-in-law's mother died, the picture was hung in the bedroom where Streeter was staying while visiting his brother. As he contemplated the back cover of *Julie's Flowers*, he looked up at the bedroom wall. Lo and behold, there was Tang's painting! More amazing is that Tang had also written lyrics to a song years prior that fit perfectly into the story. Sometimes, with the help of God, one can produce excellent work while not even being present on this planet.

Made in the USA
Las Vegas, NV
10 February 2023

67257254R00139